The Clause That Killed Him

Camden Books Publishing

José F. Nodar

The Clause That Killed Him / José F. Nodar
ISBN: 978-1-7644125-0-6 - Paperback
ISBN: 978-1-7644125-1-3 - E-Book
ISBN: 978-1-7644125-2-0 - Audiobook

Dedication

In loving memory of my wife,

Miriam Vassallo Nodar,

and her enduring presence.

You are always in my thoughts.

For anyone who's ever loved deeply, lost fully, and still found

the courage to begin again.

Table of Contents

Foreword

I first conceived of *The Clause That Killed Him* during one of my morning walks through Spring Farm and specifically when I stopped at 'the pond' (not really a pond but a water catchment) that has some benches for individuals to see and relax and watch the ducks take off and land.

This place was a favourite of my wife, Miriam, who passed away on June 10, 2025.

I will admit that I stop here and 'talk' to her just about every morning, and one morning the idea just popped up in my mind.

I was excited and returned to my home office and wrote an outline and some general sentences about what each chapter should be.

My problem started halfway through the novel when I got to chapters 12 and 13.

That was when I recognised immediately that writing a thriller set within the film industry required more than just surface-level knowledge of cameras and famous names.

To create a narrative where the conflict felt genuinely high-stakes and terrifyingly plausible, I had to treat the production process—the artistry, the logistics, and especially the contracts—with absolute fidelity.

My core conviction was this: I could not write about high-stakes filmmaking (add murder to make it even more fun) without understanding both the literal language spoken on set and the silent, lethal dangers lurking in the fine print and all the steps required in a brand launch in this industry.

The foundation of *The Clause That Killed Him* lies in the research that provided its title and central crisis. My deepest dive was into the financial and contractual traps set for high-level creative personnel.

I focused specifically on financial participation clauses. The high-risk financial clauses, particularly those involving 'net points' (a share of a movie's net profits), proved to be notoriously unreliable.

My research was primarily online, and I found some very useful resources, such as https://www.screendaily.com/ which was really helpful in understanding the basics of the industry.

I also grapple with many financial terms that are used in the industry and choose the ones that I could use easily.

If you are interested, here is a link for many of them https://www.westga.edu/ but the best one and easiest was https://www.ep.com/

Bottom line, I enjoyed writing this novella but spent more time on research than I had hoped for, but I will say it has given me the realisation that making a movie is just not pointing the camera and saying: 'Action!'

I hope you enjoy the story.

José F. Nodar

CHAPTER 1

The Ghost in the System

I hit send.

And for a moment, nothing exists except the tiny progress wheel spinning on my laptop screen.

Six months.

One hundred and eighty-four research calls.

Three private financial consultants.

Two forensic accountants.

Four nervous lawyers.

And one man who thought he owned the world.

All distilled into three hundred and ninety-seven pages.

When the email finally chimes—*File Sent*—my lungs deflate. I didn't realise I'd stopped breathing.

It's done.

I lean back in my chair and stare at the ceiling of my unit, as though waiting for some celestial authority to confirm that, yes, this is real. That the impossible manuscript with its impossible claims now sits in the inbox of Marcus Vayne, retired hedge-fund king, predator of markets, destroyer of regulation, collector of tax loopholes like rare butterflies pinned under glass.

My fingers tremble. Not with fear but with exhaustion.

Completion has a strange texture—part triumph, part grief.

The document is no longer mine, not really.

It belongs now to the trajectory of the world.

To the investors, politicians, journalists, lawyers, sharks, opportunists, and parasites who will soon devour it.

The Lattice.

The first exposé in history detailing a completely legal, globally scalable tax-evasion structure that, if fully enabled, could drain entire nations within a decade.

And I built its language.

I gave it a voice.

I leaned close to the monster and whispered it into form.

I close the laptop gently, as though setting a newborn down to sleep.

Then I rise.

My legs feel watery as I step out onto the narrow balcony of my Northport unit above the bakery shop. The evening summer heat drapes itself across my skin like warm cloth. The horizon glows orange, pink, gold—the colours of champagne bubbles and burning futures.

Every evening, my neighbour across from me waters his plants.

Tonight is no exception. He waves, and I wave back.

He does not know the world has just shifted.

Neither, for that matter, does the world.

But Marcus does.

And soon everyone will.

I pour myself a glass of cheap prosecco, the kind that tastes slightly metallic, like old coins, but tonight it tastes like validation.

I think of the first time I met Marcus Vayne.

I was still in the ghostwriter trenches then—working for CEOs who couldn't spell, billionaires who needed 'their story told,' tech founders who believed their life-altering app biographies would change humanity.

Most were harmless egotists wearing insecurity like cologne.

Marcus was different.

Marcus didn't have insecurity.

He had contempt.

Our first meeting was at a rooftop restaurant in the CBD, surrounded by men who looked like they were carved from currency rather than flesh. Marcus barely looked at me while he spoke—instead, watching the reflection of himself in the window.

I was introduced simply as 'the ghost.'

Not *Anya*.

Not a *writer*.

Ghost.

The title stuck.

In hindsight, maybe it always would.

I stare at my laptop again through the sliding glass door.

That file represents everything I've survived up to this point.

My childhood was in a house where debt was the weather.

My early twenties were spent working three jobs.

My late twenties, knee-deep in manuscripts no one would ever know I wrote.

Now, at 33, I finally feel the tectonic shift I've been chasing.

This book will change everything.

The publishing house already promised a structured bonus tied to sales performance—which, according to early international buzz, will be significant.

Marcus himself has repeatedly referenced 'life-changing numbers' as a certainty. He is a man who uses the future tense only when the future has already been purchased.

Tonight, for the first time in years, I allow myself to imagine a life without anxiety clawing at the back of my brain.

I imagine paying off my debts.

Buying a car with functioning air-conditioning.

Investing in my own projects.

Writing something with my name on the cover.

My smile widens without permission.

I deserve this.

As the sky deepens into sapphire, the first stars appear, faint as a pulse under skin.

My phone vibrates.

Marcus.

For a second, I consider letting it ring out just for the thrill of pretending I don't care.

But the childish impulse passes, and I answer.

'Marcus,' I say, injecting enough professional warmth to suggest both respect and competence.

'Just received it,' he replies.

No greeting. No pleasantries.

His voice is gravel wrapped in silk, smooth.

'Your timing is precise, Anya. Unusual for people in your line of work.'

I hear the subtext: *You've exceeded my expectations. But I won't reward you with praise.*

'Thank you,' I say anyway.

'You'll join me for celebratory drinks tomorrow,' he continues.

'Seven o'clock. Darlinghurst. The usual place.'

It's phrased as a statement, not an invitation.

'Of course,' I answer.

'Good,' he says. 'We have much to discuss before everything becomes... loud.'

The call ends.

I blink.

Not at the abruptness. That I'm used to. At the shape of his last word.

Loud.

The implication reverberates in my head like distant thunder.

Marcus doesn't say things accidentally.

A door has opened.

One I can't yet see.

A tremor of anticipation runs along my spine.

Hours later, I lie in bed, unable to sleep.

My mind keeps replaying fragments of the manuscript. Statistical models, legal loopholes, historical precedents, case studies from Luxembourg, Singapore, Switzerland, the Cayman Islands.

The genius of *The Lattice* isn't in its complexity.

It's its simplicity.

Anyone could understand it if shown properly.

Anyone could see how an entire economy could vanish into corporate tunnels, real estate shells, sovereign bonds, offshore trusts, and tax-treaty arbitrage.

Perfectly legal.

Morally horrific.

I wrote that line myself.

Marcus liked it.

A lot.

I roll onto my back and stare into the dark.

Will I regret this one day?

Giving voice to a system that could destroy nations?

No.

Because I built the exposé, not the machine.

The truth should be terrifying.

That's why it matters.

At 2:14 AM, I finally drift off.

My last thought before sleep: tomorrow, my life begins its ascent.

Morning rises clear and gold.

I wake with a strange sensation in my chest—something between certainty and hunger. I dress deliberately: sharp black dress, understated jewellery, the leather messenger bag Marcus once mocked as 'quaint academia.'

My laptop sits on my desk like a sleeping animal.

I check emails.

No messages from Marcus.

But my inbox is filling rapidly with subject lines from publishers, agents, foreign rights representatives, journalists.

I stand frozen for a second.

Then another.

It's real.

My throat tightens. I clasp my hands together the way I did as a child when my mother told me to 'hold your excitement quietly.'

God, if only she could see me now.

By late afternoon, I've reread every contractual clause, double-checked the invoice timeline, confirmed the royalty escalator figures, and saved copies of everything to an encrypted cloud vault.

I'm meticulous.

Obsessive, maybe.

Trauma does that.

Financial scarcity claws its way into your bones.

Success, once you taste even a sip, becomes oxygen.

But tonight is a celebration.

Not strategy.

I breathe slowly, intentionally.

Then I leave.

Darlinghurst at twilight is electric—vibrant, loud, flooded with glass and neon. Wealth here has an aesthetic: intentional carelessness.

Marcus chose a private lounge attached to a high-end whisky bar.

I find him seated near the balcony, alone, holding a drink like it owes him obedience.

His eyes lift as I approach.

A flicker of something.

Approval?

Possession?

Amusement?

Hard to tell.

'Anya,' he says smoothly, gesturing to the seat opposite. 'Congratulations.'

I sit.

The city hums beneath us like a living circuit.

Marcus raises his glass.

'To the ghost.'

There's a chill buried in the toast that I can't quite name.

But my glass meets his anyway.

We drink.

The night stretches ahead.

And I am oblivious—as we all are before a catastrophe—that everything I believe about tonight and about my future is about to shatter.

Like glass under a careless hand.

CHAPTER 2

The Clause

Sydney Harbour is dressed for seduction.

Its glass towers reflecting water, water reflecting stars and stars reflecting money.

Sydney can smell success the way sharks smell blood.

Marcus chose a bar that looked like it was sculpted out of steel, teak, and high-interest debt—reserved tables only, cocktails priced like minor surgery, clientele curated like a museum exhibit titled *The Wealthiest People Who Don't Feel Wealthy Enough*.

We sit on the terrace overlooking the harbour, a breeze soft as silk brushing past.

Marcus orders for both of us.

A Japanese whisky cocktail layered with smoke, citrus oil, and something volcanic.

The waiter nods as though taking instruction from a king.

When the drinks arrive, Marcus lifts his first with a posture that declares the evening a coronation—his coronation.

'To the book,' he announces.

To *the book.*
I raise my drink.
Our glasses click with a faint chime, swallowed almost instantly by the hum of the city.
Marcus savours his first sip. Then leans back, smiling.
A lion reclining after the kill.

'I must say, Anya,' he begins, swirling the amber liquid, 'you've exceeded expectations. Which in my world is not only unusual but statistically improbable.'
I force a smile.
'Thank you, Marcus.'
'Your structuring of the Cayman-Luxembourg-Singapore pass-through was positively inspired. I almost felt as if I were reading my mind.'
It's meant as praise; it sounds like ownership.
'Early feedback is extraordinary,' he continues.
'The publishing house expects unprecedented demand. Hollywood's already calling. No exaggeration.'
The words land like a thrill in my stomach.
This is the moment every ghost dreams about: to be in the room where history pivots. Where *they* stop being invisible.
Marcus takes another sip, lips pursed in satisfaction.
'And of course,' he adds, 'the franchise potential is virtually unlimited.'
Franchise.

The word hangs in the air like a prophecy.

I picture sequels, spin-offs, documentaries, maybe even panel shows.

Dare I hope even for a university curriculum

I picture revenue streams like waterfalls—flowing for decades—my name finally attached to something consequential.

Marcus watches my face. He knows exactly what I'm imagining.

That's when he laughs. Softly. Like someone about to amuse himself.

'Ah, Anya,' he says. 'There is something important we should discuss.'

My breath pauses.

'What is it?'

'The contract.'

My body stiffens.

'What about it?'

He waves a dismissive hand.

'Nothing major, I assure you. Merely a subtlety. A technicality.'

Technicality.

A word used only to excuse something sinister.

Marcus leans forward.

'You recall Section 12.4-C?'

My brain frantically scans legal hierarchies like a Rolodex thrown down a staircase.

'...not specifically.'

'Understandable,' he says lightly. It's where we define residual classifications.'

Residual.

The most beautiful word in creative law.

Add to that word the following: income, compensation, and licensing. The money that keeps arriving after the work is done.

Marcus's smile widens.

'That clause was carefully crafted,' he continues. 'It stipulates that the final payment you received makes up *a full and unconditional transfer of all intellectual property rights, including, but not limited to, future subsidiary exploitation.*'

My pulse spikes.

'I don't understand.'

'Yes, you do,' he mumbles.

He lifts his drink again.

'As per the contract, Anya, you are entitled to no future royalties, no future participation percentages, and no revenue tied to secondary rights. Under any circumstances.'

My chest hollows.

'I thought we negotiated residuals on foreign translations,' I say slowly, my voice fraying at the edges.

'No,' he replies in a firm manner. 'You thought we negotiated it.'

My throat dries.

'And film rights—?'

'Mine.'

'And documentary rights—?'

'Mine.'

'Merchandising—?'

'All mine, Anya.'

He smiles again—a small, sharp, venomous smile.

'You've already been compensated.'

I stare at him, numbness sweeping in waves through my limbs.

'But that NDA expires in three years,' I whisper. 'I still keep post-expiration credit participation—'

He interrupts with a chuckle.

'No.'

Marcus takes a slow, savouring sip.

'That's the beauty of 12.4-C. You agreed that your final payment covers *perpetual exclusion from all subsidiary income*, regardless of NDA duration.'

Regardless.

My stomach drops.

The wording flashes back into memory.

Buried in dense legal jargon and nested clauses, hidden beneath references to other references.

A legal labyrinth designed for the blind.

I run ice cold.

'Marcus,' I say quietly, struggling to maintain composure, 'this book is going to generate enormous revenue.'

'Yes,' he agrees immediately.

Not reassuringly.

Triumphantly.

'Hollywood is already circling. Agencies are competing. The buzz alone is worth seven figures.'

Seven.

The Clause That Killed Him

Figures.
My vision blurs at the edges.
'You can't expect me to just walk away from all that.'
'Of course not,' he says, lifting a hand casually.
'You'll still have a front-row seat.'
He lets that sink in.
'So, you mean…'
He finishes gently:
'You'll watch.'

Time fractures.
My mind goes silent.
A terrible stillness settles inside me.
This isn't business.
This is theft.
Not theft of words. Theft of the future.
Of life.
Marcus leans closer.
'I don't know how to put this kindly, Anya, so I simply won't try: what matters is ownership. And you own shit. You own nothing.'
My jaw clenches so hard my teeth ache.
'You tricked me.'
'Please,' he scoffs. 'You signed willingly.'
'You manipulated my trust.'
He laughs.
'Anya, my dear, trust is the currency of the naïve.'

I stare at him.

Is this real?

Is this happening?

Is this what he thinks I deserve?

'I believed,' I manage, 'that this project would change my life.'

'Oh,' Marcus says brightly, 'it will.'

He raises his glass.

'To me.'

My chest burns.

He leans back, basking in his own cleverness.

Then he delivers the final blow with a damned smirk of satisfaction.

'It'll be a $200 million franchise, darling, and you'll get none of it.'

I hear the words.

I feel each one pierce me.

Then detonate.

The harbour glitters below us.

The city dazzles around us.

People laugh, clink glasses, toast the future.

And I sit frozen, staring at a man who has just stolen mine.

In that moment, something inside me shifts.

Not breaks.

No.

Breaking implies collapse.

This is different. This is transformation.

A crystallisation.

I see him for what he is.

Not a genius, not a mentor, not a titan but a thief.

Worse, a thief who thinks humiliation is entertainment.

I straighten slowly.

Marcus is still talking, words flowing like poisoned honey, but I no longer hear him because something new has entered the room.

Resolve.

Quiet.

Cold.

Precise.

He thinks tonight was the highlight of his life. He doesn't realise it was also the last time he'll ever celebrate anything. And by the time the bill arrives, I know exactly what I'm going to do.

Strategically, perfectly, and more importantly, permanently.

I sip the expensive drink.

It tastes both like betrayal and possibility.

CHAPTER 3

The Fine Print

There's a particular silence that only comes after humiliation.

Not the stunned kind.

Not the shocked kind.

The surgical kind—where your mind keeps replaying the moment in high definition, as if it's trying to map the exact trajectory of the blade that went in.

I didn't sleep that night.

I walk into my unit, kick off my shoes, and go straight to my desk.

I don't turn on the TV.

I don't put music on.

I don't even bother changing out of the black dress that still smells faintly of smoke and Marcus's cologne.

I open my laptop.

The contract is already there.

I saved it as a PDF.

VAYNE_GHOSTWRITER_AGREEMENT_FINAL .pdf—a title that now feels like a punchline.

I scroll to the top.

Clause by clause.

Line by line.

There it is.

Section 12.4-C.

The words stare back at me, smug and unmoved.

'The Contractor acknowledges that the Final Payment constitutes full and complete consideration for all services rendered and irrevocably assigns, transfers, and waives any and all present and future claims to royalties, residuals, or subsidiary income derived from the Work and any derivative, adapted, or ancillary forms thereof, regardless of jurisdiction, format, or duration, including but not limited to motion picture, television, digital, audio, print, and merchandising rights.'

I read it once.

Twice.

Ten times.

My eyes blur, so I zoom in until the letters are huge, ugly blocks of shape and intent.

The language is perfect.

Too perfect.

Whoever drafted it knew exactly what they were doing.

This isn't clumsy exploitation.

This is art.

Legal art.

I scroll again.

There's a highlighted note from months ago— 'CHECK WITH LAWYER IF TIME.'

We both know I never did.

Rent was due.

A previous client hadn't paid on time. My laptop had threatened to die. The deposit Marcus offered for the project was more money than I'd seen in one place in years.

I told myself I'd read it properly, that I'd get a lawyer 'once the first half was in.'

I told myself a lot of things.

I didn't tell myself the truth: that I was desperate, and desperate people sign quickly.

My throat tightens, and I drag my hands over my face.

Then, I do the thing I should have done at the beginning.

I call a lawyer.

By morning, my eyes feel like sandpaper and my brain feels like static, but I'm on a train to the city, contract printed and clipped into a plastic folder.

The law firm reception smells of money and eucalyptus. Neutral art on the walls, neutral smiles behind the desk.

'Ms Sterling?' the receptionist asks.

'Yeah.'

'Tom Park will see you shortly. Please take a seat.'

I sit on a leather couch that probably cost more than my car.

I resist the urge to shred the contract in my hands.

A few minutes later, a man in his early forties steps into the foyer. Tailored suit, loosened tie, dark hair with just enough grey to signal experience but not decay.

'Anya? I'm Tom.'

His handshake is warm and firm.

We go into a glass-walled office overlooking the city. I pass him the folder with fingers that don't feel quite attached to me.

'So,' he says, flipping it open. 'You mentioned on the phone this is a ghost-writing contract?'

'Yeah.'

'And there's an issue with residual income and rights assignment?'

'Yeah,' I repeat, voice flat. 'Apparently there's none. For me.'

He gives a little noncommittal hum that lawyers seem born knowing how to make.

'Let's take a look.'

I watch his eyes move as he reads, his brow tightening almost imperceptibly at certain sections, relaxing at others.

He finds 12.4-C.

Stops.

Reads it through once and a second time.

Then he leans back in his chair and blows out a quiet breath.

There it is.

The sound of the verdict.

'So?' I ask. 'Tell me it's garbage. Tell me it doesn't hold up. Tell me there's a loophole.'

He looks at me with something like sympathy.

'Anya, I'm sorry. But this is very well drafted.'

'That's not a legal term, Tom.'

A corner of his mouth moves. 'No. But it's accurate. It's extremely specific. You didn't just assign copyright—you waived claim to *any* form of future participation.'

'Even after the NDA ends?'

'Yes.'

'So, when I'm allowed to talk about the book, if I ever decide to, I still don't own any of it?'

'That's right.'

'And foreign translations, audiobooks, film rights?'

'His.'

'Documentaries, adapted works, branded seminars, spin-offs?'

'All his. Or whichever entity he transfers the rights to.'

I grip the arms of the chair.

'But that's insane. That can't be ethical.'

He shrugs gently.

'Ethical and legal aren't synonyms. You know that, or you wouldn't be writing books about tax structures.'

I want to scream.

Instead, I say, 'There has to be something.'

Tom flips back through the pages.

'There are some ambiguities in the timeline language here and there,' he murmurs, more to himself than to me. 'But nothing that breaks the core. You got paid a fee. For which in exchange, you gave up everything else. In writing. With clear wording. And your email confirms you had time to review.

There's no evidence of duress, misrepresentation, or incapacity. I can't see a court tearing this up.'

'So, it's what?'

He meets my eyes.

'Ironclad.'

The word lands like a hammer.

'Airtight,' he adds quietly. 'Irreversible.'

Something in my chest caves in.

'Can I at least renegotiate?'

'You can *try*,' he says.

'But if he's as shrewd as you describe, he knows exactly what he has. And what you don't.'

I stare at him.

'So that's it?'

'That's the contract you signed.'

On the way home, the city looks different.

Not bigger.

Not smaller.

Just... indifferent.

Skyscrapers glint cheerfully in the sun, reflecting a world that has never heard my name.

On the train, a man in a suit scrolls through headlines on his phone. I glimpse one.

HEDGE-FUND LEGEND MARCUS VAYNE TO LIFT LID ON LEGAL TAX EVASION

My stomach turns.

On autopilot, I pull out my phone and search his name.

Article after article.

Vayne's new book is already being touted as the 'Big Short' for the next generation.

Sources say studios are circling in on what could become the most lucrative non-fiction adaptation of the decade.

Financial insiders claim the manuscript reveals a structure so legally bulletproof that it will redefine the discussion around tax reform worldwide.

My book.

His name.

My words.

His face.

The train sways gently. My vision does not.

By the time I reach my stop, something inside me has changed shape.

Back in my unit, I drop my bag on the floor and don't bother picking it up.

I stand in the centre of the living room, breathing hard.

Rage arrives in waves.

The first is heat: a roaring, molten fury at myself.

How could I have signed that?

How could I have trusted him?

How could I have believed this time would be different?

But underneath the self-directed anger, another current runs colder, cleaner.

This isn't just my fault.

Marcus knew exactly what he was doing.

He weaponised my desperation.

He weaponised the power imbalance.

He weaponised the fact that ghosts don't have leverage.

The second wave of rage is humiliation.

I see myself at that harbourside bar, dress carefully chosen, hair smoothed, heart wide open to the idea of finally belonging at a table like that.

I hear his voice.

'It'll be a $200 million franchise, darling, and you'll get none of it.'

Darling.

The way he said it. Like I was a silly child, and he was indulging me with the truth.

I press my fists into my eyes until lights explode behind them.

I want to break something. Smash a glass, a mirror, my laptop—anything to feel this fury physically instead of just mentally.

But I don't.

Under the rage, something else is forming.

Clarity.

Brutal, precise clarity.

The manuscript is worth a fortune.

Not just in money. In influence. In power. In legacy.

And Marcus believes genuinely that I am nothing but disposable labour—clever hands attached to a replaceable body.

My name will be a whispered footnote in someone's gossip column at best.

More likely, not mentioned at all.

He gets the book, the money, the fame, the film, the franchise.

I get to watch.

No.

No, I don't.

I pace.

Back and forth, back, and forth across my tiny living room, like thought made flesh.

There are moments in life when the entire story you've told yourself about who you are collapses.

I have always believed that at my core; I am lawful.

Angry, yes. Bitter, sometimes. Petty, occasionally.

But not criminal.

Not monstrous.

Not violent.

On my third circuit of the room, a new thought appears.

Quiet.

Unadorned.

Logical.

What if he weren't here to enjoy it?

I stop walking.

The air feels oddly thin.

My heart gives a single hard thump. Then another.

The Clause That Killed Him

The thought doesn't come with fireworks or dramatic music.

It arrives like a line of text in a document.

What if he weren't here to enjoy it?

I reject it instantly.

Absolutely not.

I'm not that person.

I go to the kitchen. Fill a glass with water. Drink.

I get one crazy, ludicrous thought.

Hell, he's old. Older than me. Has a lifestyle that is one-thousand percent high and high-risk. He could have a heart attack or an accident. A disappearance. A man like that slipping off the grid wouldn't shock anyone.

I grip the edge of the bench.

'No,' I say aloud. 'Stop. Don't.'

The room doesn't respond.

Because it's not the room talking.

It's me.

The version of me that is done being prey.

The ember glows a little hotter.

What would actually happen, Anya, if he vanished? If he 'retired' somewhere obscure? If he couldn't show up to sign those film contracts? If the rights needed a new, more available, more cooperative owner?

I feel nauseous.

And electric.

'People don't just disappear,' I whisper.

That inner voice, colder, more efficient, replies: *Of course they do. You wrote three chapters on how high-net-worth individuals structure disappearances. You built an entire narrative on wealthy figures moving through shell identities, offshore trusts, legal proxies.*

I stare at my reflection in the dark microwave door.

I don't look monstrous.

I look tired.

Very, very damn tired.

'What you're thinking is insane,' I tell myself.

Then I think of my bank balance.

I think of the years I've spent building other people's careers.

I think of my mother crying over unpaid bills at the kitchen table.

I think of Marcus's hand, lazy around his glass, as he told me I would get *none* of it.

The ember catches.

Becomes something like coal.

Not a plan.

Not yet.

Just the undeniable awareness that one exists somewhere if I choose to look for it.

I walk back to my desk.

Sit down.

Open my laptop.

Instead of the contract, I open the manuscript.

The Lattice: How the Ultra-Rich Use Legal Architecture to Escape Taxation Forever.

The irony tastes bitter.

I scroll to Chapter Seven.

The one about engineered withdrawals. Controlled vanishings.

I read my own words.

In certain circumstances, a strategic disappearance can be more profitable than continued participation in the visible economy.

I remember the hours I spent talking to sources about billionaires who stepped out of the public eye, leaving carefully orchestrated financial trails behind.

How the bastards changed their names, how they shifted assets–how they just deleted themselves.

I wrote the architecture of vanishing.

I exhale slowly.

The ember of murder doesn't explode. It doesn't demand.

It simply sits.

Warm and waiting.

A possibility I can no longer pretend doesn't exist.

Marcus wrote the system that lets the ultra-rich escape responsibility.

I wrote the story that showed exactly how they do it.

Maybe I can write one more thing.

A different story.

One where I am no longer the ghost in the system.

One where he is.

CHAPTER 4

The Decision

I don't so much sleep as collapse and reboot.

When morning arrives, I'm not rested. I'm suspended, caught somewhere between disbelief and inevitability. The light through the blinds is too bright. The silence in my unit is deafening.

My hands shake as I make coffee.

Not from caffeine withdrawal.

From the aftertaste of humiliation that still lingers like ash on my tongue.

I sit at the kitchen table, my coffee mug untouched, staring at the condensation forming on the glass. As if my future is dripping down and disappearing into nothing.

The manuscript file icon glints on my laptop across the room.

The ghost of everything I will never have.

I try to think rationally.

I even open a notebook.

Options: Sue

I write the word and immediately cross it out.

The Clause That Killed Him

Courts won't break a contract drafted that tightly. Tom said so. I know so.

Even if I tried, I'd lose, or I'd go bankrupt, or Marcus would crush me, and the manuscript would still be his.

Not an option.

Negotiate

The word makes me laugh.

Bitter, sharp laughter that feels like it belongs to someone else.

Negotiate with Marcus Vayne.

A man who derives pleasure from the suffering of others.

A man who thinks empathy is a technical defect.

A man who smiled as he told me I'd get nothing.

Marcus doesn't renegotiate.

Marcus wins.

Always.

Impossible.

Expose the Scheme

Here, my pen hesitates.

The Lattice isn't my invention, but its explanation, its clarity, its persuasive power—that's mine.

I could leak it.

Blow the doors off everything.

Reveal what no one is supposed to know.

Except that would kill its value and my future.

I would become radioactive in publishing.

A person who is unhireable and untrustworthy, for which the financial world would crucify me, and the legal world would devour me, and finally Marcus would sue me into oblivion.

Impossible.

I stare at the page with three options, and three specific dead ends.

I close the notebook.

The room feels smaller.

My skin feels too tight.

My thoughts circle in vicious loops.

Marcus basking in fame and applause, his face splashed across magazines, his name lauded as visionary, his fortune multiplying while I am left watching from the sidelines, in the same unit, with the same insecurity, holding the same damn debt, still nameless, and most importantly, still invisible.

He will profit from my mind forever.

My jaw aches.

I hadn't realised I was grinding my teeth.

I go to the window.

Below me, the street moves as it always does, slow, indifferent.

I imagine him five years from now being interviewed on the ABC or Channel 7 about the sequel: 'You know, the first book really changed the global conversation...'

Ten years from now: 'We always knew it would be a trilogy...'

Fifteen years: 'We're launching the educational foundation...'

Twenty years: 'We're adapting the spin-off series...'

Always him.

Never me.

The blood drains from my face.

There is a fate worse than poverty.

Obscurity in the shadow of your own brilliance.

I whisper before I can stop myself: 'This can't be my life...'

And then another option surfaces.

Not softly, not gently, but with the brutal clarity of a blade.

Remove Marcus.

I stare at the words in my mind as if I had written them on paper.

Remove.

As if the word could ever be neutral.

I mentally write the real one.

Kill Marcus.

Just thinking about it makes my stomach twist.

But I don't wipe it from my mind.

Instead, I imagine the word until letters become shapes, shapes become angles, angles become logic, and he simply disappears and the book becomes ownerless, then the rights become transferable.

Suspicious circumstances become explainable, such as an accidental death or a sudden health failure, maybe an unfortunate misadventure or what people will think is the most obvious – a voluntary disappearance.

A man like Marcus—wealthy, connected, secretive— could vanish in dozens of ways that would make perfect sense.

If he were gone, I wouldn't be nothing, and I could renegotiate everything. Then I could become the face or the voice, finally the visionary.

Not the ghost but the actual author.

He stole my future.

What would it cost to steal it back?

My pulse climbs and my breath quickens.

The idea replays again.

Not as a fantasy.

Not as wish fulfilment.

But as a strategy, it is violent. Terrifying but very logical. I walk around the unit.

Slowly, first one full circuit, then two, and then three.

The voice in my head shifts.

Not from emotion but from calculation.

Not from 'I want him gone,' but 'What if he is gone?'

What happens?

The rights halt, his estate freezes, then the publisher panics, followed by the project losing direction, and then most likely the studio pauses its plans.

And then, well, hell, someone will need to step in. Someone will need to take ownership and control the narrative while explaining the transition and of course protect the manuscript.

Someone who knows every page.

Every chapter.

Every footnote.

Someone who not only wrote the words but understands the world beneath them.

The Clause That Killed Him

Me.

My hand tightens on the back of a chair.

The idea is no longer external.

It is inside me.

It is fully formed, fully awake, and fully mine.

I sit again.

This time, not shaking.

This time, absolutely still.

'Someone has to take control,' I hear myself say.

Then: *'I refuse to spend the rest of my life watching him take credit for my work.'*

Then: *'He's already dead. He just doesn't know it yet.'*

And suddenly everything is quiet.

Clear and settled.

Not emotionally.

Intellectually.

My life is about to become something else.

Not smaller but bigger, yes, very much bigger.

The decision crystallises in my mind, sharp and perfect as iron fused with ice.

I am going to kill Marcus Vayne.

Because it is the only option left.

And because he should've known better than to laugh while he stole my life.

CHAPTER 5

Anatomy of a Perfect Crime

There are two kinds of planning.

The kind you do when you're trying not to die, and the kind you do when you're prepared to kill.

What I am doing now no longer resembles desperation or fantasy.

Or rage-driven impulse.

This is strategy.

Cold, specific, and methodical.

The way Marcus would plan.

Except this time, I'm the architect.

It begins with observation.

Marcus Vayne is not a hard man to track once you understand him.

He is predictable in the way only powerful men are predictable—he believes himself beyond the consequences of routine.

I start with the basics.

His habits.

I replay every interaction we've had. Every meeting, every phone call, every offhand remark. Memory sharpens in a way I didn't know it could. I become a forensic archivist of the past six months.

Marcus wakes early.

First, he reads the AFR, Bloomberg and the Wall Street Journal. He doesn't eat breakfast. Then, he walks in Centennial Park every second morning to play squash with a former politician. He typically arranges dinners last-minute, and he keeps a tight circle.

Marcus prefers legal loopholes to illegal risks and loves to avoid the paparazzi. He surely despises all social media because he is rich enough to be known and private enough to be unseen.

A vanishing act wouldn't seem suspicious.

It would seem inevitable.

Next: location.

Marcus lives alone in a secure penthouse, but he also owns a secluded vineyard estate in the Hunter Valley.

He mentioned it only once.

But he did.

'The estate is quiet this season,' he said, annoyed about the construction equipment delivery delay.

It is quiet, remote, and very private.

A place no one visits without invitation.

The ideal theatre.

The ideal exit.

Then comes the structural analysis.

I spend two days reading true-crime breakdowns like scripture. Doctors poisoning spouses while insurance fraud executions and disappearances executed via fake travel.

Bodies hidden, bodies lost, bodies never found.

Cases where victims simply dissolved—socially, financially, physically.

Police patterns.

Investigator blind spots.

Judicial limitations.

I take notes.

Pages of notes for things investigators always check for: motive, financials, timeline, digital activity, witness accounts, footage, phone records, bank movement, last sightings, and missing persons reports.

Places where crimes collapse because of careless digital traces, emotional overreach, visible hostility, phones carried to crime scenes, impulse-driven decisions, and panic.

Where crimes succeed because of good planning, cool heads, routine, familiarity, noise disguised as silence and finally—death disguised as choice.

Then, I study the movement of wealth.

How money evaporates.

How reputations dissolve.

How estates fracture.

If Marcus disappears, his assets freeze, then his estate triggers succession mechanisms and the publisher will halt rollout, leaving the studios to wait, and then the chaos begins. And when chaos begins, someone must manage it.

Someone must claim authority.

Someone must know the material inside-out.

Someone must speak to the press.

Someone must stabilize the narrative.

Someone like me.

***

Next, I watch documentary interviews with people who knew the vanished.

Family members described how 'he'd been acting strange lately.'

Coworkers said, 'He seemed distracted.'

Assistants admitted, 'He talked about needing a break.'

All the seeds one can plant are in the soil of expectation.

Marcus provides these seeds himself.

Overconfidence.

Secrecy.

Paranoia dressed as privacy.

The world expects moguls to burn out dramatically.

Retreat suddenly.

Disappear strategically.

The billionaire exit is an archetype.
I don't have to invent it.
I just have to utilise it.

Then, I take out a notebook.
This one is clean, uncreased, blank—just perfect.
The first page reads: 'Operation Vayne.'
I feel something settle in me as I write it.
Not darkness, not cruelty.
Control, true control.

Phase One—Psychological Architecture
1. Marcus grows erratic
2. Marcus withdraws
3. Marcus prepares exit
4. Marcus isolates
5. Marcus vanishes
All trackable. All expected and all natural.

Phase Two—Physical Opportunity
Must be private, predictable, containable, silent, close contact, non-forensic and non-chaotic.
The vineyard.

Yes.

It is perfect.

Phase Three—Aftermath Narrative

Not death, disappearance. A voluntary vanishing, a strategic withdrawal from public life.

A billionaire retreat.

These exist everywhere in global finance.

Marcus will simply become another story of powerful men walking away.

My pen moves slowly, deliberately.

Core objective: remove Marcus Vayne without suspicion.

Secondary objective: transition ownership seamlessly.

Primary threat: investigation.

Weak point: emotion.

I vow something to myself:

No emotion. Not then. Not during.

Not after.

Emotion is how people get caught. Emotion is how people confess. Emotion is the enemy of success.

I will feel nothing in the moment it matters.

That night I study Marcus's personality through a new lens—not as subject, as prey.

His arrogance is not only a flaw.

It is a lever.

His pride is not only ugliness.

It is a weakness.

His belief that he is smarter than everyone else.

A gift.

Men like Marcus do not believe they can be hunted.

Men like Marcus do not fear ghosts.

I spend three more nights researching disappearances.

I learn about: water disposal versus land disposal, body dissolution, timeline compression, biodegradable forensic elimination, decomposition mathematics, drowning intervals, vehicular staging, and the surprisingly common phenomenon of wealthy men simply walking away.

Many bodies are never found.

Many disappearances are never solved.

The more I learn, the more I understand that this can be done.

And not just done.

Done invisibly.

A perfect crime isn't flawless.

A perfect crime has flaws no one sees.

The Clause That Killed Him

By the end of the week, something shifts internally.
The idea stops being hypothetical.
It becomes structural.
A framework.
An operation.
A conclusion waiting patiently at the end of a sequence of actions.
The ember within me has changed.
It has become sharp and white.
More determined.
I sit at my desk, staring at the notebook, and whisper the truth aloud.
'He will vanish.'
And the silence that follows agrees with me.
Approves.
Encourages.
Because the truth is simple:
Marcus Vayne is already dead.
He just hasn't reached the moment of death yet.
He is walking toward it unknowingly.
Steadily.
I am simply clearing the path.

Later, lying in bed, staring at the ceiling, I imagine the future.
Three months from now.

The book launches.
The world erupts.
Media frenzy.
Financial upheaval.
Studio offers.
Global attention.
And at the centre of it all:
Me.
Not disposable.
Not replaceable.
Not silenced beneath someone else's signature.
The writer.
The visionary.
I imagine taking my place in front of cameras.
Holding the book with my name on the cover.
Speaking truth into a microphone.
And knowing with calm certainty that I liberated myself.
That I wrote my destiny, that I engineered justice, not legal justice, just real justice.
And the world will applaud me for it.
Without ever knowing why.
Without ever knowing whom I had to remove to get here.
Ghosts don't commit crimes.
Ghosts take what they are owed.
Even if they must steal it back from the living.
Bit by bit, plan by plan, step by step,
I am becoming something new.

Not a ghost.

Not prey.

Not background.

I am becoming the invisible architect of someone else's final chapter.

And my first real one.

CHAPTER 6

Enter The Lattice

I used to think the most terrifying thing in life was ignorance.

Now I know better, for it is knowledge. Knowledge you can't unlearn. Knowledge that could ruin worlds. Knowledge that you gave to a man who smirked as he stole your life from under your hands.

Tonight, that knowledge sits in front of me like a loaded weapon.

I open the file on my laptop–the one labelled innocuously as 'Draft Notes Chapter 14.'

My chapter and his secrets.

The Lattice.

I scroll slowly, reading words that were mine, though his name sits beneath the final draft.

When I wrote this, I thought I was building meaning. I thought I was telling the story behind the empire.

I didn't realise I was architecting a confession.

And now I read it like a manual for war.

The Clause That Killed Him

The Lattice was Marcus's genius or, rather, the part he pretended was genius while using me like a power tool.

An invisible web straddling authority trusts within trusts, charities funnelling into subsidiaries, subsidiaries funnelling into holding companies, holding companies that owned property through nominee directors so far removed from him that even God would need clearance to trace the paperwork.

You could look straight at it and never see him.

A ghost made of gold.

He had explained it to me once, walking the length of his penthouse like a professor drunk off his own brilliance.

Now I read the words.

My words.

And I understand the genuine horror.

I didn't just understand *The Lattice*.

I built the language of it.

Each paragraph describes a loophole, with each sentence being a breadcrumb trail through the dark.

Marcus called it 'a masterpiece of legal engineering.'

I called it—once—a miracle.

Now, I call it the perfect crime.

And suddenly I see it differently.

Like a surgeon revisiting a body she once tried to save, knowing now she must figure out where the arteries weaken and where the bones fracture and the blood pools.

Because the trick of *The Lattice* was not in its construction.

It was in its vulnerability.

Pressure points hold together every unseen system. Find them, and everything collapses.

My fingers tremble as I highlight the section that outlines Cayman transfers.

I remember writing it.

Marcus leaning behind me, one hand on the back of my chair, the other swirling his whiskey.

'You have a sharper mind than you let on,' he had murmured.

Back then, I'd been young enough to mistake that for praise.

Now, the memory is acidic.

Because I realise something he never intended:

The Lattice is airtight externally.

But internally?

It is delicate.

And I was the only person who ever mapped its skeleton honestly.

Which means I am the only person alive who can dismantle it without leaving a single trace.

I stand, pacing, for the room is too small for what I'm thinking.

I press my hands to my mouth as a laugh escapes—a sound that frightens me.

Not hysteria.

Something colder.

Sharper.
Like a blade being unsheathed for the first time.

To kill a man like Marcus, you don't shed blood.

You erode power. His financial power, his reputational power, and his institutional power.

You erase the admiration that shields him like armour.

If Marcus disappeared tomorrow, *The Lattice* would keep him wealthy even in death.

But if *The Lattice* imploded, or the regulators descended?

But if the shareholders panicked or if the wrong people learned the right things?

He wouldn't just lose money.

He would lose the throne beneath him.

He would be naked.

An ordinary human.

Oh, God.

A thrill pulses through me.

A dangerous one.

Because for the first time, I can see the shape of justice.

Not in courts, not in interviews, or in op-eds or accusations.

But in pressure.

Silent.

Steady.

Merciless.

Marcus thinks no one in the world understands his system well enough to weaponise it.

He's correct.

Almost.

There is one.

Me.

And perhaps that is fate.

Or irony or something far more primal—something ancient and vicious.

Poetic justice.

I drag a fresh notebook toward me.

Blank page.

Blank future.

A battlefield.

I write two words: *THE LATTICE << TARGETS >>*

Then beneath:

1. Nexus Accounts
2. Philanthropic shell trusts
3. Leverage nodes
4. Risk thresholds

Each one a pulse point, a potential fracture line, a future blade.

As the ink sinks into the paper, I feel something inside me coalesce.

The Clause That Killed Him

Resolve, purpose, and certainty.

Marcus built a machine of ghosts and gold.

I built the language that made it myth.

Now I will turn that language into the scripture of his downfall.

The Lattice gave him power.

And *The Lattice* will take it away.

Because I am done being his architect.

From this chapter on, I become his undoing.

CHAPTER 7

The Bait

There's a particular type of lying that feels like performance art.

The type of performance art where every tone, every pause, every breath must be deliberate.

Tonight, I become an artist.

Marcus won't come to me.

He wouldn't grant me the dignity.

So, I create a reason for him to want me.

I rehearse the script in my head twice, maybe three times.

Not too eager, just valuable.

I call him.

The phone rings longer than feels polite.

He answers without a greeting.

Typical.

'Marcus,' I say, voice steady, calm, businesslike.

Silence.

Then, a measured exhale.

'Anya. This is unexpected.'

He doesn't sound pleased or inconvenienced.

Good.

Fear sharpens me more effectively than caffeine ever could.

'I've been revisiting the manuscript,' I say.

'Have you?'

Flat, controlled. Already bored.

'Yes,' I continue. 'And I've found something.'

A small, strategic pause.

'A direction we didn't explore the first time.'

That gets him.

I hear the slight shift in his tone, interest prickling through irritation.

'What kind of direction?'

Time to pull the knot tight—slowly.

'You told me once that what separates a bestseller from a phenomenon is narrative mythology,' I say.

'A new myth.'

He doesn't interrupt.

I press forward.

'I think I've found it.'

A longer silence this time.

Calculation.

'What are you talking about?'

I smile—careful he won't hear it.

'What if,' I say softly, 'we could transform the book from a financial exposé to a prophetic warning about the future of global wealth? A kind of blueprint of what comes next?'

A gamble, and a specific one.

Marcus cares less about money than about empire.

And an empire needs prophecy.

His curiosity tightens around me like a wire.

'Explain.'

I lower my voice, forcing him closer despite the distance.

'I'd rather do it in person.'

'That's unnecessary.'

'It's complicated. And confidential. And I think you'll want to see the material for yourself.'

That sells it—the illusion of substance.

The promise of exclusivity.

And most importantly, the implication that without him, it means nothing.

He hates nothing more than missing out.

'We'll discuss it next week,' he says.

'No,' I reply, injecting urgency.

'This is time sensitive.'

A risk.

He hates being told what to do.

But he hates the idea of losing leverage even more.

Another pause.

Long enough for me to hear my pulse against my teeth.

Then, quietly:

'When?'

I exhale internally.

'Tomorrow night,' I say. 'Your Hunter Valley house. I'll drive up.'

He considers this.

The Hunter Valley estate is remote.

Private, a fortress in the middle of vineyards and bushland.

He built it for secrecy.

He trusts that space.

Perfect.

He finally says, 'All right. I'll have security open the gate. Seven-thirty.'

The old me would have thanked him.

'Very well,' I answer. 'See you then.'

He hangs up without a goodbye.

But I'm already smiling.

The moment the line goes dead, I drop the persona like a heavy coat.

My legs give out, and I sit on the edge of the bed, shaking.

Not fear.

Not yet.

Adrenaline.

The kind that buzzes under the skin, like electricity waiting for thunder.

In less than thirty minutes, Marcus went from unreachable to intrigued.

From sceptical to hungry.

Because I fed his addiction: legacy.

And legacy always devours caution first.

I stare at the map pinned over my desk, *The Lattice* diagram, printed in sections, taped together like some conspiracy theorist's fever dream.

It is no longer an analysis.

It is a strategy.

And tomorrow night will be the first move on the board.

Marcus believes he invented the game.

But I designed the language the game speaks.

I stand, draw a line through the page labelled *Marcus: untouchable* and replace it with a new word:

VULNERABLE

And below it...

BAIT TAKEN.

For the first time since he gutted my career with a single contract clause, I feel power humming in my bones again.

Power that is dangerous, addictive, and righteous.

Tomorrow the war begins.

I like my new personality.

CHAPTER 8

The Estate

The Hunter Valley always looks like a dream someone forgot to finish.

Rolling green hills stretch under a wash of sunset gold.

Vines whispering in long, perfect rows.

The quiet hum of the warm evening air slips across the land like silk.

Beautiful, serene and untouched.

Ideal if one wants to vanish or make someone else vanish.

The closer I drive, the more the landscape appears to recede, like the world pulling gently, politely, away.

Giving Marcus room, giving power room, and giving secrets room.

The last fifteen minutes of the drive are gravel and dust, the road narrow enough to make me feel as if civilisation is politely excusing itself from responsibility.

By the time the estate is in view, twilight has deepened everything into a rich, dangerous bruise.

The gates, tall, black, and silent, open remotely before my car reaches them.

As if summoned by intention rather than invitation.

The estate emerges like a shadow carving itself into existence: sprawling vineyards, a gravel courtyard, manicured hedges, steel, and stone architecture perched arrogantly above the land—as if daring the earth to try to reclaim it.

The air is warm and thick and utterly still.

Marcus always loved control.

Even over the weather, if he could manage it.

I park beneath the portico, where the concrete gleams like marble despite the dust the wind kicks across it.

The front doors open before I knock.

Marcus stands there, holding a crystal decanter and two glasses.

'No traffic?' he asks without greeting.

'No.'

He hands me a glass.

Far less than he pours into his own.

His shirt is open at the collar; he's barefoot, comfortable, confident.

More sphinx than man.

Inside his house smells of money, age, and oak–a scent deliberately curated to feel dignified rather than decadent.

He built it like a mausoleum for wealth.

He gestures for me to follow, but I get the distinct impression any protest would roll uselessly off the walls.

We go to his favourite living room.

Floor-to-ceiling windows look out onto endless vineyard rows swallowed by darkness. The horizon catches the last sliver of dying sun.

He pours again.

His glass spills slightly.

He doesn't care.

'So,' he drawls, settling deep into a leather armchair that probably cost more than my old apartment, 'you said you found something.'

He says it with annoyance, like I've interrupted his coronation.

'It's complicated,' I reply.

'Everything is,' he says, waving a hand. 'Especially genius.'

He smirks as if expecting laughter.

He used to intimidate me.

Not anymore.

He sips deeply—too deeply.

The alcohol rolls off him in waves.

And then he begins:

'The studio from L.A. wants a trilogy,' he announces.

'No vision, obviously, but they're willing to pay obscene numbers. Meanwhile, a UK network is foaming at the mouth for a prestige adaptation. Six episodes. Lavish. Expensive.' He grins wide, wolfishly. 'British guilt is very profitable.'

He laughs at his own joke.

I stare.

He keeps going.

'And the Germans,' he says, leaning closer, voice lowering like he's sharing a secret, 'are begging for documentary rights. Begging. They want to chronicle me.'

Not the work, not the story, not the system.

Him.

His ego swells as the whisky drains.

The more he drinks, the more he becomes a caricature of himself, grandiose and ravenous for admiration

'You're surprised?' he says, catching my silence and misinterpreting it.

'Of course you are. You always underestimated what this project meant. What I meant.'

He taps his chest with two fingers.

As if greatness is a birthmark.

As if he's owed adoration by virtue of existence.

'When I started this,' he continues, 'people laughed. Called it insane. Told me no one cares about a book on financial architecture.'

He leans back, waving one hand dismissively.

'But once I put my touch on it? Once I shaped it? It became transcendent.'

My arms stiffen.

'Your touch?' I repeat.

He waves again, amused.

'Oh, come now. You provided vocabulary. Structure. Pages. But the myth, that's me.'

He grips the glass harder.

'And now look at us,' he adds, motioning between us with a derisive tilt of his drink.

'I'm on every financial podcast in the world. And you are well. You're here.'

The meaning hangs in the air like smoke.

Like a slap coated in velvet.

I swallow the bitterness rising in my throat.

He smirks, pleased by my silence.

He loves silence. Loves forcing it out of people.

He gets up, moves behind me, leans over the back of my chair.

Close, too close.

His breath smells of whisky and arrogance.

'You know,' he murmurs, 'you never would've lasted in the spotlight. You're not built for it.'

I keep my gaze fixed on the window.

He lowers his hand to my shoulder, fingers brushing lightly.

Possessively.

'Not resilient enough,' he continues, voice dipping into something altogether different.

'Not ruthless enough. You break. I thrive.'

His hand lingers.

The moment is humid.

I stay still, but not because I'm frozen.

Because I'm studying him.

Like a surgeon studying the final incision.

He moves away, pacing again, agitated by energy too large for his skin.

'Honestly, Anya, you should be grateful,' he says, pouring again.

'Without me, you'd still be writing copy for tech start-ups.'

Grateful.

It rings in my ears like a gunshot.

He keeps going.

'You know what your problem is?' he asks suddenly.

I don't answer.

'You think the world owes you something,' he says, pointing at me with the rim of his glass.

'Because you're clever. Because you work hard. Because you have "talent."'

He makes air quotes.

'News flash,' he sneers, 'talent is common. Winning isn't.'

He waits for me to respond.

I do not.

Which frustrates him.

Good.

Very good.

He sits heavily, watching me like a bored predator.

'I built everything. I earned everything. I deserve everything,' he says.

A long pause.

'And some people,' he adds, eyes narrowing slightly, 'are better off staying in the shadows.'

As he speaks, I imagine every fragile node in *The Lattice*.

Every pressure point.

Every vein of gold waiting to rupture.

Marcus doesn't realise he's bleeding arrogance all over the room.

He thinks cruelty is strength; he believes dominance is invulnerability, and he believes humiliation proves superiority.

Tonight, I remove those beliefs.

The Clause That Killed Him

One at a time.

Like ribs from a skeleton.

There is a particular shift that happens when monumental decisions crystallise.

It doesn't feel dramatic, not explosive, not operatic.

It is quiet, surgical, and cold.

A moment in which the world stops feeling unpredictable and becomes instead—sharply, painfully lucid.

As Marcus taunts me, drinks, boasts, mocks the very ground he thinks I'm kneeling on—even as he slurs in a way that suggests he views me less than a peer and more as a woman trapped in his orbit—

I feel the shift.

Like a blade sliding home.

No hesitation, no fear, no second thoughts, just certainty.

Not tomorrow, not after more planning, not once I gather more intel.

Tonight, I pull the first thread. Tonight, I begin the process that will unravel everything he has built. Tonight, I weaponise every piece of knowledge he thinks he owns, and tonight, Marcus Vayne stops being untouchable.

I sip the whiskey I have not drunk.

He finishes another glass.

The room darkens.

The vineyards disappear into the night.

The Lattice gleams behind my eyes.

Tonight, the empire starts to die.

And Marcus Vayne will never—ever—see it coming.

CHAPTER 9

The Method

There is a strange quiet that settles inside a person when the decision is no longer theoretical.

It doesn't tremble; it steadies. A cold, crystalline stillness.

The silence winter makes when snow falls.

That fills me as Marcus finally passes out.

Not slumped, just gone.

Face-first across the leather sofa, one arm dangling, glass on the carpet, shirt half-open, breath sour with whiskey and triumph.

The titan at rest.

And so profoundly breakable.

I stare at him for a long time to confirm.

He is unconscious.

He will not wake quickly.

And I am ready.

Not emotionally, because emotion has nothing to do with what comes next.

This is an operation. This is surgery, and this is inevitability.

The balcony door is open—the night breeze curling fingers of cold into the room.

I walk out and confirm what I already knew—there are no security cameras inside nor outside.

The vines below are little more than darkness and outlines, the world softened by the late hour.

The balcony railing is waist-high and made of a sleek metal.

Modern and simple.

The kind of architectural flourish designers love.

And coroners see often.

An accident waiting for a moment to be born.

I turn and look back inside, through the glass.

Marcus remains unmoving.

Somewhere in the back of my mind, a voice whispers: *He will destroy countless others if you don't do this.*

I don't answer.

I don't have to, for my conviction is already complete.

I move through the house without haste, without emotion clouding my limbs.

Just precision.

It's remarkable how easily the body behaves when the mind stops doubting.

His laptop sits open on his desk, lid glowing faintly with the screensaver.

His phone rests charging beside it.

His tablet, expensive and unnecessary, is on the sideboard like an afterthought.

Marcus, the arrogant and cheap bastard, had thought no one would ever pierce his sanctuary.

Power always forgets vulnerability.

I begin with the devices.

I do not destroy; I do not tamper. I just cause an erasure.

Curated absence.

I remove only what matters: communications related to the manuscript, specific legal documents, emails between him and me.

Not all of them, only enough to blur certainty; just enough to suggest irrelevance, distance, and detachment.

Enough to make the world shrug and move on.

Then I add to the illusion: a series of browser searches that paint a picture. A playlist of drinking songs queued carelessly. A half-written email to no one that makes no sense.

Signs of loneliness, of indulgence, of a man spiralling privately.

A binge weekend.

One no one was meant to witness.

The whiskey bottles in the dining room are full.

Were full.

They won't be by the time I leave.

His fingerprints will be on every one of them.

Mine will not.

I check the glasses.

Only his has residue.

Mine has never been touched.

The Clause That Killed Him

I leave it.

Intentionally.

He wouldn't pour me more than he thought I deserved.

Let the world know.

Even in death, let him expose himself.

I return to him and find him still unconscious.

Breathing steadily.

Completely unaware of the architecture collapsing around him.

I take in the details of his face, his arrogance gone slack and his calculation dissolved.

He looks so ordinary, so small. Frail, even.

As though the myth has evaporated and left only flesh behind.

I do not feel victory. I feel clarity and necessity.

He ruined lives with signatures, destroyed people with clauses, crushed futures with indifference.

Tonight, the scale shifts.

I kneel beside him.

My hands tremble faintly—not from fear.

Relief.

The operation begins.

Not with violence. With planning, angles, alignment, trajectory, and impact.

A stumble can be a tragedy.

A railing can be so treacherous, and gravity can be cruel because, as everyone knows, drunkenness can be fatal.

Especially alone, especially unwitnessed, especially at height.

I whisper nothing.

I pray for nothing.

I simply perform the task.

And afterwards I arrange the scene.

The glass by the door, the spilled whiskey, the balcony chair slightly askew.

The fragile illusion of a fragile man losing balance.

It is disturbingly quiet work.

Methodical.

Like organising a bookshelf.

There is no blood.

No weapon.

No outrage.

Just inevitability.

When I am done, I stand back and observe the tableau.

It looks like sadness; it looks like excess; it looks like consequence and, crucially; it does not look like me.

When the narrative is sealed, I collect my bag, and I walk to the door.

I do not look back.

There is nothing left for me inside this house.

I unlock my car, slip inside, turn the ignition, and in that moment the night exhales around me.

Tonight, Marcus Vayne vanishes.

And tomorrow, the world will believe it was the alcohol, the solitude, the stumble, and the fall. And the cruel indifference of gravity. Not the work of a ghost.

A ghost he created himself.

Me.

CHAPTER 10

The Vanishing

In the aftermath of decisive action, the world goes strangely quiet.

Not around you—around *within* you.

The mind, previously a battlefield of fear and adrenaline, becomes a glass lake.

Still. Silent. Reflective.

The night air clings to me as I drive back to my unit, but the stillness inside remains unshaken.

Marcus is no longer a problem.

Now comes the aftermath.

The transformation.

The crafting of his last act.

Because tonight was about creating a narrative.

One that would eclipse suspicion.

One so believable, so aligned with the man the world believes Marcus Vayne to be that no one would even consider murder. They would accept the more obvious truth. I will give them the truth.

That Marcus finally did the most Marcus thing imaginable and ran.

I pull into a roadside rest stop at 1:17 a.m.

An hour from the estate.

No cameras, no traffic, no prying eyes.

The perfect nowhere.

I open my laptop and tether to my phone.

Not my number, of course—a burner.

Marcus isn't the only one who sees opportunity where others see limitation.

The first phase is digital, invisible, mathematical. Like the President of the United States in 2026 loves to say: 'Beautiful. It is beautiful.'

I log into the first portal using the authentication token I retrieved months ago while he was too drunk to notice what I copied.

He assumed competence protected him.

Ignorance actually would've.

Marcus always mistakes arrogance for armour.

The offshore account dashboards load slowly—languidly, like old millionaires reluctant to rise.

Cayman Islands, then Cyprus, then Luxembourg and finally Singapore.

Each one built through the very architecture I helped create.

I withdraw only *some* funds.

Not all; it would be too obvious and too dramatic.

Just enough to imply deep fear and a rushed escape.

Enough to suggest that disaster is coming, and Marcus knows it.

Forty-three million through three different accounts.

Offsets, transfers, and delays.

Invisible threads I pull taut.

The numbers vanish from balances and reappear in different pockets of the web—the kind that require knowledge, not force, to locate.

I move them in shapes only Marcus should understand.

Triangles, loops, and spirals.

Like *The Lattice* itself.

The world has always believed he was escaping something.

Now, he finally does.

***

The second phase is psychological.

Narrative engineering. My favourite form of writing—what I do best.

I open his email from my laptop, simple enough, given the recovery codes he left unprotected.

Marcus always assumed that anyone close to him would never become dangerous.

He mistook subordination for loyalty.

I compose three emails.

Two to his lawyers, one to his CFO, and each short and abrupt.

Typical Marcus.

Cryptic enough to inspire panic.

We need to talk immediately. Something has come up.

Sent at 2:14 a.m.

Freeze internal movement. Temporarily stepping away.

Sent at 2:15.

No calls. Secure channels only.

Sent at 2:16.

Then I delete the drafts, delete the deletions and I close the laptop.

Phase three.

Messaging.

The burner phone is quiet in my lap, its glow the only artificial light for kilometres.

I open his encrypted chat app and send two messages to the one friend the media knows he trusts.

The friend the newspapers always call his 'confidant.'

The friend who secretly hates him.

Marcus: *You were right. Regulators are circling.*

Marcus: *I'm leaving for a while. You won't hear from me, but you'll understand soon.*

I leave the chat open, as if in haste.

Phase four is public perception.

I pause and steady myself.

Marcus always said the most convincing lies were the ones based on truth.

So, I use the truth.

I log into his secondary social account.

Not the public-facing one.

The private one only corporate insiders knew existed.

Low followers.

High influence.

A developed and cultivated audience of sharks.

Exactly the demographic that *knows* how men like Marcus behave under pressure and believe they would do the same under the same circumstances.

I post a message—ambiguously alarming.

Sometimes walking away is the only leverage left.

Not profound, but perfectly Marcus.

I schedule deletion for 48 hours later.

Not fast enough to seem accidental.

Not slow enough to seem planned.

Exactly enough time to seed speculation.

And from speculation, panic.

The fifth phase is cleanup.

Marcus's downfall must seem voluntary.

Predictable.

Like the climax everyone always suspected but didn't want to speak aloud.

The Clause That Killed Him

Marcus Vayne's vanishing isn't shocking.

It is inevitable.

Just like this:

1. regulatory pressure
2. financial scrutiny
3. offshore liquidity movements
4. erratic messages
5. intoxicated isolation
6. sudden silence

I haven't created a mystery.

I've created an answer.

One the world was already prepared to accept.

It's funny, Marcus always believed we crafted a legacy together.

He never realised I was crafting an exit.

I close the laptop.

It is 3:06 a.m.

Dawn is still hours away.

I sit back in the driver's seat, tilt my head against the rest, and exhale slowly.

I am calm, unburdened.

Not triumphant and not broken.

Simply finished with the hardest part.

In movies, they show panic as shaking hands and spilled tears and breakdowns.

But we know that real life is colder, cleaner, and quieter.

The Clause That Killed Him

The mind is sharper when the deed is complete.

I watch a truck pass in the distance, headlights carving a brief silver trail across the highway.

Then darkness again.

Then silence.

The sixth phase is departure.

Not escape—departure. I am simply leaving, with caution.

With calculation, obviously, but with no trace of haste.

No desperation and no erratic behaviour.

That is how guilty people move.

I am not guilty.

The world will believe Marcus vanished willingly, recklessly, and predictably.

And the mechanisms that sustain public belief are simple:

1. narrative
2. timing
3. motive
4. absence

He will provide all four.

His history already does most of the work.

All I have to do is reinforce the foundations.

As I start the engine and drive back toward civilisation, I reflect:

For all his brilliance, Marcus never considered that the greatest vulnerability in any system is the person who designed it.

He should have known.
He trusted my mind more than anyone's.
And yet he never saw me coming.
Because he never thought I mattered.
That was his fatal flaw.
The belief was that he was untouchable.

As the first light of dawn bleeds into the sky behind me, I realise something profound:
Marcus is not gone.
His body is still there.
The estate is still standing.
The official search has not begun.
The phones have not rung.
There will be hours before anyone notices.
Perhaps a full day, maybe three.
Vanishing doesn't happen the moment you disappear.
It happens slowly.
Over time, like erosion.
Like forgetting, and by the time they realise he will already be myth.
His own myth.
I have merely sharpened the edges.
Tomorrow, the rumours will begin.
Soon, the speculation and eventually, the panic.
And finally, the acceptance.
The empire won't die instantly.

It will rot.

Collapse inward, decay, silently but with dignity.

Like old money, like legacy, and like a ghost.

And then what remains?

Me.

Not triumphant, not exalted and definitely not celebrated.

Simply free.

Free of the contract, free of the humiliation, free of the cage, free of Marcus and for the first time since this began, I breathe without trembling.

Tonight, I was a ghost, and tomorrow, I will be someone new.

Someone Marcus could never imagine, someone he should have feared.

Not the apprentice, not the assistant, not the voice behind the curtain, but the architect of the myth, of the empire, of its destruction.

And now of its disappearance.

Marcus always said the greatest victory wasn't in winning.

It was in controlling the narrative.

He was right.

And now?

That narrative belongs to me.

CHAPTER 11

Rewriting Reality

The first thing I learn about reality is that it doesn't have to be true.

It just has to be consistent because people don't examine consistency.

They relax into it, and I'm counting on that.

By the time the news cycle begins its slow pivot towards Marcus, by the time 'concerned colleagues' start noticing he hasn't answered emails, by the time his lawyers leave messages with that thin edge of irritation turning into worry—my work is already several steps ahead.

I am not trying to outrun the story.

I am trying to write it.

The 'contract' lies on my kitchen table.

It looks entirely unremarkable.

It is laser-printed, stapled, in black ink with 12-point font.

Just paper.

Just words.

Just one more legal document in a world drowning in them.

But it is, in essence, my resurrection.

The header bears the name of a perfectly respectable-sounding holding company—a shell I formed three months earlier when this plan was still embryonic and terrifying even to think about.

'ORPHEUS IP PTY LTD.'

A little private joke.

Orpheus, who went into the underworld to retrieve something he loved.

I am not rescuing Marcus; I am rescuing myself.

The document is a Rights Assignment Agreement.

Pages of dense, unsexy language.

Whereas, whereas, whereas.

Definitions, clauses, carve-outs.

All of it meticulously, surgically tailored from previous contracts I wrote—real ones Marcus signed with real partners.

I know his cadence on paper.

His preferences.

The lawyer he liked.

The phrases he would always insist on were: 'exclusive, irrevocable, worldwide, in all presently known and future media, and throughout the universe.'

His vocabulary was ostentatious even in legalese.

I mimic it perfectly.

I am, after all, his ghost.

The date on the contract is six weeks ago.

Well before his 'disappearance.'

Well before anyone will claim to have last seen him.

A quiet, private deal, executed between a man who wanted to diversify his assets and an IP company fronted by a 'consultant' he trusted.

Reasonable, unremarkable, boring and reality's favourite shape.

At the bottom of page seven, just above the signature line, is the crux:

Assignor hereby transfers, assigns, and conveys to Assignee all right, title, and interest in and to the manuscript currently titled THE LATTICE *and all derivative works, adaptations, and ancillary rights thereto...*

Followed by a neat subclause about revenue streams, backend participation (for him, of course), and the explicit statement that creative control rests with the Assignee.

With me.

Invisible behind a corporate name.

Forging his signature wasn't the hardest part.

I had watched him sign documents for years.

The lazy flick of the *M*, the arrogant loop at the *V* in Vayne, the small downward pressure on the pen when he crossed the final letter.

I'd asked once why he always used the same pen.

He'd smirked and said, 'Consistency reassures people.'

He was right.

I practiced on scrap paper for days.

Not obsessively.

Methodically.

Until I could mimic the shape and rhythm.

The minor tremor at the end of the stroke that came from his slight impatience.

When I did the final version, my hand was perfect, with no shaking whatsoever.

His name looked back at me from the paper.

Marcus Vayne.

Assignor.

Beneath that, the tidy, restrained signature of 'A. Mercer, Director, Orpheus IP Pty Ltd.'

Me.

And a notarisation stamp from a jurisdiction that never met a piece of paper it didn't adore.

Bought, not earned.

Reality doesn't care.

It's mid-morning when I walk into the agency office.

Not his office—the agency that handled the initial book deal.

Frosted glass, polite carpets, a woman at reception with a neutral smile, and the watch you buy when you need people to know you can.

'Can I help you?' she asks.

'I have documents for Eden Ross,' I say.

The primary agent.

The one who'd always taken my notes but never my name.

She hesitates and then recognises me.

'Oh—Anya, right? From the Vayne project.'

There's a moment where this could go wrong.

Where she could ask too many questions.

Where she could remember too much.

Instead, she simply smiles, with a touch of sympathy in it.

'I heard things got complicated,' she whispers.

'Yes, they did.' I reply.

She buzzes me in.

Eden's office smells like expensive coffee and tired hope.

He's on the phone, gesturing for me to sit as he wraps up a call with 'a nightmare producer' in L.A.

He hangs up, rubs his temple, and offers a tight smile.

'Anya. Been a while.'

'Yes,' I say. 'Sorry for ambushing you.'

'We're used to ambushes.'

He waves at the chair.

'What can I do for you?'

I take the contract from my folder.

Laid, not thrust. Polite and controlled.

'I wanted to update you on the status of the manuscript,' I say.

He frowns.

'I'm not sure that's—'

'Marcus assigned the rights to my company. Before he left.' I cut in gently.

I slide the document across the desk.

He takes it with the reluctant curiosity of a man who spends his life reading lies dressed as opportunity.

His eyes skim the first page, then slow.

His posture shifts.

I watch the exact second his brain clicks into legal mode.

He flips.

Reads.

Re-reads.

The silence stretches.

'How long ago was this?' he asks, eventually.

'Six weeks,' I say. 'He wanted to step back a little. Focus on other ventures. Less public, more diversified.'

Eden huffs a tiny, sceptical laugh.

'That doesn't sound like Marcus.'

'It sounded like the version of himself he thought he'd become,' I say.

That lands.

Marcus had been complaining about the 'circus' for months, especially when drunk.

How the media reduced him to bite-sized quotes.

How everyone wanted a piece.

How exhausting it was being brilliant in public.

Eden had heard all that too.

'He asked me to take over the creative shepherding,' I add. 'Quietly. He didn't want the story to be about him anymore. Just the work.'

I see something shift on Eden's face.

Not belief, not yet.

But alignment.

The story I'm telling matches the man he knew.

Eden flips to the signature page and then pauses.

Runs his thumb lightly over the stamp.

'Is this notarised?'

'Yes.'

'And the assignment is total? This is everything?'

'Yes,' I say again.

'Rights, derivatives, all media. He has a participation clause. It's in his interest for the book to succeed. He just didn't want to be visible.'

Eden reads the clause.

'Of course,' he murmurs.

'Of course he kept participating.'

A tiny, wry smile.

If this were fake, he thinks, Marcus would never have allowed such generosity without a back end cut.

Conveniently, it isn't generous at all.

It's perfect.

Eden leans back, staring at the ceiling for a moment.

'We've been trying to reach him for days,' he says.

'It's unusual. Even for him.'

I nod, expression carefully measured.

Concerned, but not alarmed.

'Maybe he's already gone?' I suggest softly.

'He wouldn't vanish without telling us about something like this,' Eden says, tapping the contract.

'Wouldn't he?' I ask gently.

We both sit with that.

Because the truth is, Marcus absolutely would.

That's his brand.

Unpredictable, brilliant, and self-serving.

If this were a stunt, it would be exactly on-brand.

If this were real, it would still be on-brand.

'You'll need to loop Legal in,' I say.

'I just wanted to make sure you weren't blindsided when you hear things from other people.'

'Other people?'

I hesitate, letting the silence thicken just enough.

'There are rumours,' I say at last.

'That he knew investigations were coming. Offshore structures. Regulatory pressure. He mentioned "getting out ahead of it" a few times.'

I look down, then back up, as if I've said too much.

Eden's jaw tightens.

'That's not unexpected with his history,' he drawls.

'Exactly,' I say.

I stand.

'I won't take more of your time. I just wanted to put the paperwork on your radar. If Marcus resurfaces and wants to renegotiate...' I shrug. 'I'm open to conversation. In good faith.'

'Of course,' Eden says automatically.

He's already thinking of the angles.

Protect the asset, protect the income stream, and protect himself.

By the time I leave the building, he will have emailed Legal, forwarded the contract, and attached a single, telling line:

This tracks with things Marcus hinted at a while back.

Reality rewritten in real time.

Not by me.

By them.

Seeding rumours isn't as hard as people think.

You don't need a megaphone.

You need the right whisper, in the right ear, at the right time.

I start with a junior publicist I know from a festival panel.

Someone bright, ambitious, hungry for gossip that makes her feel connected to the big leagues.

We meet for coffee.

I tell her I'm 'concerned.'

I say I heard Marcus talking about 'getting out before the next wave hits,' and 'not wanting to be the face of a scandal.'

I let the words 'tax haven' drop once, casually, like an afterthought.

I don't push.

By that evening, she had told three other publicists and one journalist she swears she didn't name.

By morning, the journalist had messaged a contact in London.

By lunch, someone in a film development office sends a cautious email to a colleague: *Have you heard anything about Vayne going off grid to dodge a probe? Might affect option talks.*

The beautiful thing about Marcus's reputation is that I don't have to invent anything wild.

I just emphasise what everyone already suspects.

That he built his empire on edges so sharp they cut, that he played with structures regulators don't fully understand yet, that he's smarter than the people chasing him.

If a man like that disappears after a weekend of heavy drinking on a remote estate, what's more plausible?

An accident on a balcony?

Or a calculated vanishing act?

The answer doesn't have to be right; it just has to be compelling.

By the end of the week, the first article appears.

Not in a major outlet.

Not yet.

A niche financial blog with a name like *Global Ledger* runs a speculative piece:

'Is Maverick Billionaire Author Marcus Vayne in Trouble?'

'Unconfirmed reports suggest the controversial financier may face renewed scrutiny over his offshore holdings.

Sources say Vayne has been "unreachable" for several days. Some insiders speculate he may be "lying low" in a friendly jurisdiction...'

I stare at the screen. I didn't write those words.

But I did.

I didn't speak to that journalist.

But I did.

Reality is a collaborative hallucination, and I merely nudged the first domino.

The rest, predictably, is human nature.

Fear, greed, ego, and storytelling.

By the time a more respectable outlet runs a shorter, more cautious piece, the framing is already set:

Amid rumours of regulatory interest, sources say Vayne had recently discussed 'stepping back from the spotlight' and 'allowing others to shepherd his work.'

I know exactly which 'source' provided that line.

Her name is Eden's assistant.

She thinks she's protecting the agency.

She thinks she's contextualising.

In truth, she's corroborating my fiction.

Turning it into fact.

At night, when the noise of my phone quiets and the world spins on its own without my intervention, I sit at my desk and look at the original notes I wrote for the book.

The Clause That Killed Him

The early drafts, the clumsy metaphors, and the scribbled diagrams.

Back when I still believed this project would be the thing that made me.

Not unmade me.

Not reshape me into something unrecognisable.

I run my fingers over the pages.

I think about the word *ghostwriter.*

It was always meant as an insult when said with a certain tone.

Invisible, exploitable, disposable.

Now, it feels like an evolution.

Ghosts move through walls; ghosts see what the living don't, and ghosts are feared because they don't obey the same rules.

I've stepped out of the margins and into the story.

Not as a character but as the author.

Reality bends around authors.

It always has.

Marcus understood that and weaponised it.

He built myth; he harvested belief, and he manipulated what people thought was true until it became indistinguishable from fact.

I learned from the best.

And now I've done what every apprentice eventually must. I've surpassed him.

The world will, in time, come to accept the official version: Marcus sensed danger. He shifted assets; he sold off certain rights; he slipped into the cracks of the global system he once glorified, and he became the ghost he always threatened to be.

Some will say he died.

Some will say he's sipping rum on a private beach, watching headlines with amusement.

Some will insist he's planning a triumphant return.

None of it matters.

What matters is this: on paper, in law, in contracts and agreements and agency systems, the book is mine; the film is mine; the adaptations are mine; the story is mine.

And for the first time since I signed that cursed original contract, since I let him own my work, my labour, my voice, I feel the world tilt just slightly back toward balance.

Not justice.

There is no justice here.

Just reclamation.

Just survival.

Just a woman rewriting reality until it finally, finally includes her.

CHAPTER 12

The Launch Team

There is a moment after an empire collapses where the world looks for a survivor to crown.

Not because they care, not because they want justice, but because they need a story.

Nature hates a vacuum, and publishing despises one.

Marcus's absence leaves a crater.

Silence that stretches like a fresh wound through the industry.

Booksellers call agents, then producers call publishers, then foreign rights teams call lawyers.

Everyone smells disaster.

Which means everyone wants a solution.

And I have arrived just in time with exactly that: a book, a message, a face, and a saviour.

And a myth crafted with surgical precision.

It begins with a phone call from Eden two days after the first rumour pieces hit the trade blogs.

He tries to be calm but fails.

'Anya,' he says, 'this might be bigger than we thought.'

Oh, I think.

I know.

Publishers want to speed up the new version of the launch.

A faster schedule.

More visibility.

A *hero narrative.*

'There's interest,' he says, meaning *bloodlust.*

'From whom?'

He lists names I spent years hoping would look at me.

They finally are.

But not because I became brilliant overnight.

Because I became inevitable.

'When can you come in?' Eden asks.

I pretend to check my calendar: 'Tomorrow morning.'

The conference room looks different from the last time I was here.

Then, I was a footnote, but today, I'm the room's gravitational centre.

Six people greet me.

Coffee brewed fresh, bottled water lined neatly, and their smiles suggest sympathy, but their eyes suggest hunger.

This is where the real work begins.

A woman steps forward in a sleek dress, sharper mind, a voice honed for influence.

Nadine, the PR strategist.

'Anya,' she says warmly, shaking my hand as if we've known each other for years. 'It's an honour.'

She means: *You're our next product.*

I smile.

'I appreciate the support.'

She sits beside me instead of across.

An ally.

At least for now.

'We need to talk about how to position you,' she says.

Ah, now it starts. The branding of a human into a commodity.

'Your role in the book,' she continues, 'is now central.'

The others nod.

They smell a phenomenon.

Not just a release.

A movement.

'The narrative is simple,' she explains. 'You discovered the truth. You exposed it. You paid a price. And you're telling the world, so others don't suffer the way you did.'

She pauses.

'Marcus became the distraction. But *you* are the message.'

I almost laugh because the irony is delicious.

Marcus believed he was the message.

He believed he *was* the myth.

He believed the spotlight was a birthright.

Now it is a weapon.

One pointed in my direction.

But I hold the grip.

'What do you need from me?' I ask.

Nadine tilts her head, assessing something deeper in me.

'We need you cooperative,' she says. 'Authentic. Intelligent. Emotional when appropriate. Controlled when necessary.'

Controlled.

Yes.

That part won't be a problem.

'We need you ready,' she continues, 'to embody the role.'

'And what role is that?'

Her smile widens brilliantly constructed.

'The truth teller.'

Her voice softens.

'The woman who risked everything to reveal a system designed to crush whistleblowers.'

Whistleblower.

The word settles like a stone in my chest.

Not because it's untrue, but because it's almost true. Close enough to resonate and far enough to protect me.

Nadine outlines the media plan.

Major interview outlets, editorial features, magazine profiles, and festival keynote appearances.

A carefully timed explosion of attention.

All anchored to one idea: Anya, alone, brave, and correct.

A moral crusader, a reluctant hero.

A woman who stared into the abyss of global corruption and spoke the truth anyway.

That version of me will sell, and I will let her.

Truth and myth are not opposites.

They are partners.

Myth is just truth with sharper edges.

By the end of the hour, there is already a publicity machine being assembled around me.

A communications schedule, with a press kit and a talking points sheet.

A crisis brief.

Not about my involvement—of course not—about Marcus.

If he 'returns.'

If he 'denies.'

If he 'refutes.'

The language is subtle.

Supportive and ambiguous enough to be credible.

Firm enough to maintain my position.

'We won't antagonise him publicly,' Nadine explains.

'You respect him. You're saddened. But you're determined to bring transparency to this space.'

Marcus would choke on the irony.

The man who built an empire on secrecy will be remembered for inspiring a movement of transparency.

This is poetic justice with huge profit margins.

That afternoon, they fitted me for a wardrobe.

Clean, while sharp and minimalist.

'Your aesthetic must communicate clarity. Integrity. Strength without aggression.' Nadine says.

Clothes as narrative, hair as narrative and even makeup—more natural, less defensive—is narrative.

It's all theatre, but theatre is what shapes cultural consciousness.

Marcus knew that, for he built spectacle, and he commodified intelligence, and finally he weaponised mystery.

I'm simply following the blueprint, but with a better ending.

The press leaks begin slowly.

Then speed up.

Suddenly, I am everywhere.

Selectively.

Strategically.

'She discovered a labyrinth of global corruption.'

'She stepped into the spotlight only after Marcus disappeared.'

'She never wanted fame.'

'She wanted justice.'

Whistleblower, expert, and truth-teller with words like armour, words like prophecy and with words that rewrite the past into something noble.

At night, alone with the glow of my lamp, I re-read the first article that calls me: 'A courageous insider.'

I laugh quietly, not because it's false, because the world finally understands two truths: power is always taken and never given.

And history isn't decided by the powerful.

It's decided by whoever writes the final draft.

I close the laptop and lean back, letting the silence settle around me.

I built the story; I constructed the evidence; I shaped the perception, and now I am shaping myself.

The launch team is merely amplifying what I already sculpted.

Nadine said it best: 'You're not replacing Marcus. You're eclipsing him.'

He always feared irrelevance more than death.

And now, at last, both belong to him.

And neither belongs to me.

Not anymore.

Now I am the author of the truth, or at least, its most compelling version.

CHAPTER 13

Hollywood Bites

The first sign that things have escalated beyond anyone's expectations is the email subject line:

OFFER—CONFIDENTIAL / URGENT

Then another.

And another.

The offers pile up in my inbox like live grenades.

I stare at them in disbelief for a solid three minutes before opening the first.

A L.A. studio.

Big, loud, and expensive.

They want not just the film rights but the trilogy rights. To a book that, two months ago, was effectively stolen from me but now it is a miracle and a curse.

Because every step forward tightens the noose.

Not around me but around the lie.

Around the delicate, intricate structure I've built.

If one thread comes loose, everything unravels.

So, I play it calm and controlled.

As though I've been preparing for this my whole life.

When, in truth, I feel like I am standing on the edge of a cliff wearing glass shoes.

Eden calls me within the hour. He sounds giddy, almost panicked, but sober in the way only greed makes a man sober.

He says, 'We're in a bidding situation.'

I say, 'Already?'

He says, 'Yes. The buzz is insane.'

I reply, 'Let's not rush.'

He is so thrilled by those three words that he almost drops the phone.

Because only someone with leverage says: *let's not rush.*

Marcus taught me that.

Reluctance is currency, interest is control, greed is power and most importantly fear is leverage.

I swallow the rising panic and say what Marcus would have said:

'I want to see what the market does.'

The silence on Eden's side is reverent.

It is worship.

'Oh, God,' he whispers. 'You're great at this.'

If he only knew.

Hollywood is chaos dressed as glamour.

They don't just want stories; they want worlds, and they want to own them.

Body, bones, blood.

They send pitch decks, mood boards, comparable titles, P&L projections and even projected streaming numbers.

One studio promises a prestige mini-series with an Oscar-winning director attached, while another promises theatrical box office and a marketing rollout 'to rival the Nolan machine,' a third promises everything.

They know nothing about me.

But they want everything from me.

My calm replies are brief and measured.

Thank you for your interest.

We are considering multiple proposals.

I look forward to reviewing more concrete terms.

In reality, I don't know how to read half the language they're using.

Ancillary rights? Backend points? Profit participation waterfalls?

I feel like I am deciphering alien glyphs.

So, I learn fast, brutally, and obsessively.

I read books, articles, contracts, and even old deal memos.

Every night I turn legal jargon into equations or variables with logic and the instinct for survival.

I am building a new lattice, not of offshore accounts but of opportunities.

Profits, and power, and the best part is that this time, the architecture belongs to me.

Phone calls start at 5am Sydney time.

London agencies, Paris film funds, Munich independent producers and then L.A. calls begin around midnight.

By day 5, I have slept nine hours total.

My voice is sandpaper, my pulse is caffeine, my nerves are violin strings, but my performance, oh my performance, is flawless

Because fear, when mastered, becomes fuel.

And the deception beneath everything grows more complex with every agreement, every promise, every headline.

The narrative must be airtight, and the myth must be unassailable.

Marcus cannot return.

The world must believe this was always the plan. He stepped back, and I stepped forward.

'The student surpasses the mentor.'

They are already saying it; they are eager to believe it because it has shape and symmetry, and justice.

Stories need justice.

Even when life does not.

Especially when life does not.

Nadine coaches me between meetings.

'You don't need to be fearless,' she says. 'You just need to seem fearless.'

I nod. I am terrified. But I am also focused.

She drills posture, breathing, eye contact, and narrative beats.

'Hollywood doesn't buy books,' she says.

'They buy myth.'

And Marcus was myth personified.

Until he wasn't, and now, I must be the unlikely hero, the reluctant truth-teller, the woman who risked everything to expose a global inequity machine.

We rehearse that line.

Until it sounds like breath.

Until I can say it anywhere, to anyone, with a straight spine and soft eyes.

Even though the truth is far more complicated.

He was cruel and careless; he believed admiration was permanence; he believed power was infinite; he believed he was safe, and he taught me everything that would destroy him.

On day 12, a major American studio offers something I never imagined I'd see attached to my name: guaranteed green light.

Meaning they'll make the movie no matter what.

No hesitation, no hedging, no development hell.

No 'maybe in three years.'

Production.

Locked.
And I am the consultant.
The voice of authority, the expert on global corruption, and the intellectual heroine.
The irony burns like whiskey in my blood.
The thing Marcus wanted most I just inherited.
Without him, because of him and now despite him.

That night, alone in my unit, surrounded by papers and offers and strategies, I stare at myself in the window.
My reflection is unfamiliar.
Harder. Sharper.
Not aged but refined.
My pulse steadies.
The fear is still there, but it has changed its shape.
It now lives beneath determination, under purpose.
I am terrified because I know the truth with every deal I sign.
With every interview I give, with every stage I step onto, I must become more perfect.
I must be very careful to ensure I make myself invulnerable.
My deception must be immaculate; hell, it has to be flawless and bulletproof; it has to be perfect 100% of the time.
Because I cannot falter.
Not now.
Not when everything is finally within reach, not when the world has finally turned to face me.

I fold the studio offer and place it on the table.

Right beside the forged contract that made everything possible.

And I say quietly, under my breath: 'Stay ahead of the truth.'

Because the truth is a predator, and I intend to outrun it.

CHAPTER 14

A Detective With Questions

The news broke sooner than I had expected.

Three days after the vineyard and I carefully erased him and three days after I became the ghostwriter of a manuscript whose author has, officially, vanished.

I knew this moment would come, but the human body doesn't prepare for inevitability.

It responds as if the surprise is fresh each time.

My phone rings.

I don't recognise the number, and I stare at the screen for three long seconds, long enough to feel sweat prickle under my hairline, before answering.

'Hello?'

A pause and then a calm, controlled voice:

'Ms Sterling?'

'Yes.'

'This is Detective Sergeant Elise Monroe, Sydney Police. I'm following up regarding a missing persons report you may be connected with.'

There is no tremor in her voice.

No struggle and no hesitation for professionals; they do not flinch.

And predators do not roar—they purr.

I swallow.

'I see. Yes, of course. A missing-persons report. How can I help you, Detective Sergeant Monroe?'

'Thank you. I'd like to ask you a few questions,' she continues.

Not an invitation. A procedural step she already knows I'll comply with.

'When would be convenient?'

I inhale and say the only acceptable answer.

'Now is fine.'

'I'll be there in thirty minutes.'

Very precise, like she planned for me to say yes.

The line disconnects.

The unit feels suddenly smaller.

As though the walls have leaned in, curious and hungry.

I straighten, nothing. I don't rehearse because rehearsal means anxiety; anxiety leaves footprints.

I instead sit on my couch and drink water slowly, letting calmness become physical.

Control starts in the body, and I know if my hands are steady, my voice will be steady.

Fifteen minutes later, I hear the knock.

When I open the door, she is exactly as I expected. In her forties, lean, contained. Eyes sharp but not predatory. Oh no, not yet.

More like someone mapping a landscape before stepping into it.

Her hair is tied back, and she wears minimal makeup.

Her clothes are practical, dark, professional without trying too hard.

She offers a badge instead of a handshake.

'Detective Sergeant Elise Monroe.'

'Please come in.' I nod.

She steps inside with a kind of quiet confidence.

Assessment.

Her type doesn't rush to conclusions. They go through possibilities like stepping stones.

She sits at my dining table without waiting for instructions.

'Thank you for seeing me on short notice,' she says.

'It's no problem.' I sit opposite her.

She slides a small notepad out of her bag and clicks a pen open.

Lovely, so old-fashioned. This way, I can see the questions.

She wants the silence between them.

'Just to clarify,' she begins, tone even, 'you wrote Marcus Vayne's upcoming book?'

I nod.

'Well, ghostwrote,' I correct gently. 'It's his material. I structured it.'

'And the book is complete?'

'Yes.'

'When was the last time you saw Mr Vayne?'

I breathe in, breathe out.

'Five days ago.'

'Where?'

'At a bar on the harbour.'

'What was the nature of the meeting?'

'Celebratory,' I answer. 'We toasted the completion of the manuscript.'

She writes slowly.

'Did he appear stressed? Overwhelmed? Worried?'

I shake my head and add: 'No. Quite the opposite.'

'Describe his state.'

I let myself smile faintly and say: 'Triumphant.'

She looks up.

That catches her interest.

'How so?'

'He believed this book would change everything,' I say.

'For him. For the financial world.'

'And for you?'

I let a small, self-deprecating laugh escape.

'I'm just the ghostwriter. The spotlight was always his.'

She studies me.

Not suspiciously but thoughtfully.

Then she continues with another question.

'When you parted ways, did he indicate he was travelling?'

Here, I allow ambiguity, a carefully measured ambiguity.

'He... implied he might step away for a while,' I say. 'But not explicitly. Not detailed, but he hinted.'

She waits in silence, and I fill the silence because silence is danger.

'I took it to mean he wanted time to decompress before the launch. You know—disconnect, reflect.'

She nods slowly.

'So, if he disappeared voluntarily, in your view, it wouldn't be shocking.'

'No,' I say calmly. 'It wouldn't, but I would not call it a disappearance. I am sure he has done it before, but I do not know.'

She studies me again, and I can feel her mind turning over gears.

She closes her notebook.

'Thank you, Ms Sterling. That helps. We may contact you again.'

I nod politely.

'Of course.'

But she doesn't get up.

Instead, her eyes drift to my bookshelf, to the manuscript binder sitting closed beside my printer, to the glass of water sweating rings onto my table.

Then back to me.

'When you were with Mr Vayne last,' she asks softly, 'did he seem like a man preparing to start something?'

I think about the irony.

The cruel, perfect irony.

I answer carefully.

'Yes.'

She tilts her head.

'And did he seem like a man preparing to end something?'

For half a second, half a heartbeat, I freeze.

She notices.

Of course, she notices.

She was watching for that.

I recover with a small, forced laugh.

'I mean, Marcus always seemed like a man finishing something, beginning something. He was always planning six moves ahead.'

'Hmm.'

She rises with the same calm motion, the same measured energy.

'Thank you for your time.' And I let her out the door.

The moment the door closes, my knees weaken just slightly.

She is dangerous, very damn dangerous.

Because she is not satisfied and she already feels the shape of a story that isn't quite right.

Because she is asking questions no one else is asking yet.

Across town, in a cramped office lined with cold case boxes and burnt-out fluorescent lights, Detective Sergeant Elise Monroe stands before a whiteboard.

Two junior detectives sit across from her.

Constable Jodie Hammond and Senior Constable Liam Sharpe.

Both clutching coffee cups and both bleary-eyed from long shifts.

It's late afternoon.

Monroe draws a clean line down the whiteboard with a marker.

'Timeline,' she says.

Sharpe speaks first, flipping through notes.

'Marcus Vayne, last confirmed visual contact: housekeeper, Monday morning.'

Hammond taps her tablet.

'And pinged a cell phone tower near Glenbawn Reservoir three days ago.'

Sharpe adds: 'Bank accounts inactive since. No withdrawals. No credit activity.'

Hammond adds: 'No calls. No emails. No new travel bookings under his name.'

Monroe writes:

Glenbawn Reservoir, 6:47 PM, last signal.

She pauses and then writes beneath it: Three days missing.

'Who reported him missing?' she asks.

Sharpe consults the report.

'Two sources: housekeeper and publisher.'

Hammond frowns.

'That's odd.'

Monroe nods.

'Very.'

Sharpe asks, 'What's the significance?'

Monroe taps the board.

'Clients rarely vanish right before a career-defining book launch.'

Sharpe leans back.

'So, you think this disappearance is connected to the book.'

Monroe answers carefully.

'I think everything is connected to the book.'

Hammond scrolls through a dossier.

'The manuscript covers a legal tax-evasion structure that could undermine entire regulatory frameworks.'

Sharpe whistles low.

'People kill for smaller financial stakes than that.'

Monroe holds up a printed document.

The ghostwriter contract summary.

HIGHLIGHTED.

Hammond reads aloud: 'Ghostwriter transfers all rights, access, and future income to Marcus Vayne. Permanently.'

Sharpe blinks.

'So, she gets nothing?'

'Not a cent,' Hammond replies. 'Even after the NDA expires.'

Sharpe tilts his head.

'Christ. He cut her throat and then handed her the napkin.'

Monroe writes on the board:

Ghostwriter: ANYA STERLING

Underlies it twice.

Sharpe asks, 'Did you meet her?'

Monroe nods and takes a sip of her coffee.

'Smart. Careful. Contained.'

Hammond raises a brow and states: 'Guilty?'

'No. Not guilty and not innocent either.' Monroe says immediately.

Sharpe frowns.

'She admitted they celebrated together. That he was triumphant.'

'Triumphant,' Monroe repeats, tasting the word.

'She emphasised that,' Hammond observes.

'Deliberately,' Monroe adds.

Sharpe leans forward.

'What does triumphant imply?'

Monroe uncaps the red marker.

'This.'

She writes in big letters:

NO REASON TO RUN.

Hammond speaks slowly.

'So, if he had no reason to flee...'

Sharpe finishes: 'Someone else might.'

Monroe's eyes flick up.

Not triumphantly.

Not eagerly.

Thoughtfully.

'Disappearances this total,' she says quietly, 'rarely happen without help.'

Heavy silence.

Hammond then asks: 'You think Anya Sterling helped him disappear?'

Monroe shakes her head and explains: 'No. I think someone wanted him gone.'

Sharpe exhales.

'And you think she might know something.'

'Yes, and I think she knows exactly how high the stakes are.'

I sit staring out my balcony window, watching the city swallow itself in amber dusk.

Knowing she is not finished, not even remotely.

Detective Sergeant Elise Monroe is not the kind who files paperwork and moves on.

She is the kind who hunts loose threads.

And Marcus Vayne left a tapestry full of them.

I sip wine slowly and deliberately.

I remind myself that I built a disappearance with every component being precise and every timestamp intentional with every trail curated.

But even the perfect crime depends on perception.

Narrative.

Belief.

Which means her belief must be guided, directed, and managed.

Because suspicion is weed like. If you let it root, it will spread, and if you let it grow, it will devour.

But I remind myself of something crucial: I am not afraid.

Fear is for prey.

I am something else entirely now. Something sharper and more deliberate, more prepared.

Marcus always thought he was untouchable; he always believed no one could reshape his future but him.

But in the end, I rewrote him.

And now?

If needed, I will rewrite her too.

CHAPTER 15

A Leak in The Lattice

The first sign that something is wrong isn't an email from Legal.

It's a notification from X.

I still have the app only because the publisher begged me to 'lean into author visibility.'

Normally I ignore the app.

This morning, the notification preview catches my eye.

Is this @AnyaSterling's book or someone else's stolen playbook? Asking for a friend with a few billion in assets and a very good legal team. #TheLattice

Attached is a screenshot of a headline from a finance blog.

'RIVAL HEDGE-FUND LEGEND CLAIMS, "THE LATTICE" STEALS PROPRIETARY STRUCTURES'

My body goes cold.

I open the article, and the name mentioned hits me like a slap.

Viktor Lang.

If Marcus Vayne was a shark, Lang is a deep-sea leviathan. He is older, quieter, infinitely more dangerous.

He runs a fund rumoured to own parts of governments.

The man regulators 'consult' with before proposing reforms, just to make sure they won't accidentally upset the real owners of the world.

Lang is the type of individual you do not screw around with.

The article is thin on detail but thick on provocation.

Sources close to Viktor Lang say he believes several mechanisms outlined in the upcoming book 'The Lattice' mirror a proprietary internal white paper circulated within his firm five years ago. Lang is said to be exploring legal options, including injunctions, defamation claims, and IP theft litigation. Sterling's publisher declined to comment.

I stare at the screen, and my first thought is: *Of course, Marcus stole from someone else.*

While my second thought is: *Shit, they're going to come for me.*

My third thought is, unhelpfully: *Crap, I did not plan for this.*

The kettle whines on the stove.

I don't remember putting it there.

The phone rings before the whistle peaks.

I know who it'll be, and I answer anyway.

'Anya,' Julian says, no hello.

'Tell me you're awake and sitting down.'

'Mostly,' I reply.

'So, you've seen it.'

'The Lang piece? Yeah.'

He exhales a sharp, strained breath.

'Okay,' he says, tone shifting into professional mode.

'We're in crisis-prep. Legal wants you at the office in an hour. Can you do that?'

An hour!

'Sure.'

'Okay, bring any research notes you have. Source materials, interview transcripts, anything that supports originality.'

The absurdity of it almost makes me laugh.

Originality, as if anything in that manuscript could be described as original except the way I arranged and weaponised the truth.

'Okay,' I say again.

'And Anya?'

'Yes?'

'Don't answer questions online. Not even a joke. Not even a like. Today, you're invisible unless we put you in front of a camera on purpose.'

I almost say I'm very good at being invisible, but I just murmured, 'Understood.'

We hang up.

I lean my head against the kitchen cabinet.

So far, the plan has accounted for police, family, housekeepers, journalists, and internal corporate fallout.

I did not account for a rival billionaire screaming, 'Marcus Vayne stole my toy' through the press.

I suddenly hate all of them with a purity that almost makes me dizzy.

Marcus and Lang and everyone who sits atop piles of money and treats the law like a menu.

I slam the kettle off.

Time to move.

I pull out the folder with printed research notes, the external hard drive with interview recordings, and the encrypted USB with Marcus's original drafts and spreadsheets. My hands tremble only once.

I tell myself: *This is good. This is leverage.*

If Lang is claiming ownership, then Marcus is exposed as a thief.

If Marcus is exposed as a thief, the world will view him as compromised, unreliable, deceptive.

Which makes his sudden disappearance far more likely to be perceived as flight than as murder.

I can still use this if I survive it.

The publisher's meeting room feels smaller today.

There are six people at the table: the publisher himself, Alan; General Counsel, Hannah; and the external IP lawyer, sleek, quiet, unnamed. Also add the Head of Non-Fiction, Maria. Of course, then there is Julian, PR, and little ole me.

For some reason, I am the only one without a blazer.

My notebook feels like a shield that's too small.

Alan starts.

'Okay,' he says, fingers steepled, 'let's get the obvious out of the way. We all know about Lang's threat. We expect something formal within twenty-four to forty-eight hours. Possibly an injunction filing.'

'On what grounds?' I ask, even though the article made it obvious.

'Claiming that significant parts of the structure described in *The Lattice* mirror a proprietary internal document,' Hannah answers crisply. 'He'll say you or Marcus had access to it and therefore misappropriated confidential intellectual property.'

'I never had access to anything belonging to him,' I say immediately.

Hannah's gaze sharpens.

'Good. We need that on record. Preferably in writing.'

'What about Marcus?' Maria asks. 'Could he have seen this white paper?'

Alan snorts softly.

'He's been in that world for decades. If Lang sneezed near a tax treaty, Marcus was probably there when the handkerchief came out.'

Not helpful, I think.

Accurate, but not helpful.

The unnamed external lawyer finally speaks.

'Legally,' he says, 'what matters is whether the expression of the idea was copied, not whether the idea itself overlaps. You can't copyright a tax concept. You can copyright the way it's documented.'

'So, we need to prove independent development,' Hannah summarises.

'Correct.'

All eyes slide towards me.

My mouth is suddenly dry.

'Walk us through your process,' the external lawyer says.

'How did you build the architecture of *The Lattice*?'

I inhale and exhale.

'I started with Marcus's initial thesis,' I say. 'The idea that there existed a multi-jurisdictional, entirely legal structure embedded in existing treaties that could be strung together.'

'And the details?' Hannah presses.

'We went jurisdiction by jurisdiction,' I reply.

'I cross-referenced public filings, academic papers, legal commentary, tax rulings. Marcus provided some anonymised examples. I interviewed two tax lawyers, one retired regulator, and a consultant who specialises in treaty arbitrage.'

'Names?' the external lawyer asks, already poised to write.

I rattle them off. I kept meticulous notes.

Meticulousness now feels like a lifeline.

'Did you and or Marcus ever mention Viktor Lang to each other?' Julian asks quietly.

I hesitate.

Once.

Marcus had called him 'that sanctimonious old reptile.'

But that's not what they're asking.

'Not in relation to the book,' I say. True enough. 'We talked about other players, but not him.'

'Is there any possibility,' Hannah asks, 'that Marcus had access to a confidential Lang document and incorporated it into the book?'

The room waits.

I force myself to look thoughtful, not frightened.

'Marcus never showed me any documents branded with Lang's firm,' I say. 'He sent me spreadsheets, emails, his own notes. If he was channelling someone else's work, he didn't tell me.'

'So, in your professional opinion,' the external lawyer clarifies, 'what you wrote is a synthesis of publicly available information and proprietary insights provided by Mr Vayne as your client.'

'Yes,' I say.

'And you did not knowingly reproduce any proprietary documents belonging to any other fund.'

'No.'

He nods.

That was the first test.

I passed for now.

Hannah leans forward.

'If this goes to court,' she says, 'you will be cross-examined by people who make a sport out of shredding witnesses. They're going to dig into every email, every draft, every note. Is there anything, anything at all, you haven't told us that could undermine our defence?'

There is a murder, I think.

There is a dead man and a vineyard and a carefully orchestrated disappearance.

But as far as they're concerned, we're talking about copyright.

So, I meet her eyes and say, with full, steady honesty about this question:

'No.'

Julian glances at me.

There's a flicker of something like pride in his expression.

'Okay,' Alan says.

'Then from our side, we hit back hard. We emphasise Anya's rigorous process. We point out that Lang cannot own a concept. If he saw early drafts through some leaked channel, he may have reverse-engineered our structure and is now claiming prior art.'

'That's bold,' Maria mutters.

'Well,' Alan says dryly, 'if he's going to accuse us of theft, we don't have the luxury of timidity.'

The external lawyer raises a hand.

'Caution,' he says. 'Lang's pockets are deeper than this entire company's market cap. We push too hard; he sues not just for an injunction but for damages. Our best outcome is to establish that any overlap is coincidental, or that both parties independently derived similar structures from publicly available baselines.'

'So, we play scholar,' Julian summarises.

'We talk about convergent thinking under similar global incentives. We frame Anya as the one brave enough to expose what men like Lang and Vayne have been doing for decades.'

Hannah nods slowly.

'That's one angle.'

Everyone looks at me again.

'How confident are you?' the external lawyer asks, 'that you can defend the content intellectually in interviews? If we put you in front of experts, can you speak their language?'

And there it is —the freaking minefield.

The façade.

I know this world.

I've spent months decoding jargon, unspooling complex mechanisms into language the average intelligent reader can follow. But that's translation, not invention. If a hedge-fund quant pounces on a technicality, I have a narrower margin than Marcus would.

I take a breath.

'I'm not a tax attorney,' I say.

'I'm a communicator. My role has always been to distil complexity into something legible. But I understand the architecture. I can walk people through it. I can explain the mechanisms at a conceptual level, and I have the receipts for our sources.'

Hannah studies me.

'What if they want to dig into equations? Specific treaty subsections?'

I'm honest.

'I can prep. But if you want a pure technical slugfest, bring in one of the consultants we interviewed as an independent expert. Let me be the storyteller. People don't fall in love with equations. They fall in love with narratives.'

Julian smiles faintly.

'Which is why,' he says, 'we should lean into her voice, not shove her behind a tax lawyer.'

The external lawyer shrugs.

'Optically, having the author front and centre is good. Legally, we add a technical expert to the line-up, so she's never left alone on an island.'

'Make it happen,' Alan says.

Then to me: 'Anya, you'll likely be asked about your relationship with Marcus. Lang's team will want to paint you as his accomplice or his puppet. We need you to be clear that you are neither.'

Accomplice.

The word tastes acidic.

'I was his writer. Not his co-conspirator.' I strongly state.

Hannah raises a brow.

'Do you believe he could have taken something from Lang?'

I give the only answer that doesn't make me look either stupid or complicit: 'I believe men at that level borrow freely from each other's unspoken playbooks. If Lang claims ownership over structures that exploit legal gaps created by governments, he's identifying as part of the problem.'

Julian's eyes gleam.

'There's your quote,' he murmurs.

The external lawyer scribbles something while Hannah slowly closes her folder and comments: 'Okay. For now, we are going to prepare a letter of demand. Anya, we will collate your sources. We secure all drafts and communications with

Marcus. And we do not, under any circumstances, acknowledge wrongdoing.'

The meeting breaks.

As we file out, Julian touches my arm lightly.

'You did well,' he says.

'Did I?'

'You didn't flinch,' he says. 'That's half the game.'

He doesn't realise that's because I've already survived a far worse cross-examination.

From myself.

The minefield begins two days later.

First, a panel call with three 'independent experts' the publisher brings in to stress test our content.

Two former regulators and one academic in international tax law.

All men, all older and all radiating a quiet disdain for non-technical people who dare to speak in their domain.

We're on video.

They don't bother hiding the fact that they expected Marcus, not me.

Professor Hartley blinks at his screen.

'I must say,' he begins, 'I assumed Vayne would lead this discussion.'

'He's not available,' Hannah says smoothly from off camera.

'Anya has a full working knowledge of the material.'

'Hmm.' He adjusts his glasses, which I've already decided are pretentious for reasons that aren't entirely rational.

Regulator Number One, Mr Keane, clears his throat.

'The central claim in your book,' he says, 'is that by chaining specific treaty provisions across districts, one can achieve effective zero taxation while remaining fully compliant. That's not new.'

'I disagree,' I reply, voice steady.

'Pieces of it exist in various reports and case studies. What's new is exposing the pattern as a cohesive architecture, and mapping how players like Vayne—' I flick my eyes deliberately to the camera '—and, presumably, Lang, operationalise it.'

He frowns.

'But the structure you describe between the Dutch conduit and the Luxembourg hybrid entity is very similar to something that appeared in an internal industry paper several years ago.'

Internal industry paper.

Lang's ghost raises its head.

'Similar how?' I ask.

He squints.

'The sequencing. The debt-pushdown.'

'Treaty order dictates sequencing,' I say.

'There are only so many ways to chain them. That multiple people can arrive at the same path doesn't make that path proprietary. It makes it efficient.'

Hartley interjects, informative-like.

'But, Ms Sterling, surely you understand why those of us who've spent our lives inside this system might be sceptical of a narrative-driven book claiming to reveal something groundbreaking.'

Inside, my irritation spikes.

Narrative-driven.

Translation:

You're just a writer.

'I understand scepticism,' I reply.

'That's why every chapter has references. You'll find rulings, case law, public filings. You're not being asked to believe me. You're being asked to look at what's already there and admit what it adds up to.'

Silence.

Keane exchanges a look with Regulator Number Two.

Hartley softens—barely.

'And you are confident you can defend this against a challenge from someone like Lang?'

There it is.

The test, so I hold his gaze.

'I am confident that Lang doesn't own the law,' I say.

'And I'm confident that if he believes exposure of his methods constitutes theft, that's a confession, not a defence.'

Hannah mutes her mic just long enough to murmur, 'Nice,' off-screen.

By the time the call ends, my spine aches from holding my posture so straight.

But they didn't break me.

They saw a façade; they didn't see the cracks, and they surely didn't see the body buried under the vineyard soil.

That evening, an email arrives.

Subject line: RE: Police Follow-Up – Vayne

My heart stutters.

It's from Detective Sergeant Monroe.

Ms Sterling,

Thank you again for your time the other day. I have a few follow-up questions regarding Mr Vayne's professional relationships. I understand from public reports there is now a dispute with a Mr Viktor Lang concerning the content of the book you wrote for Mr Vayne. I'd like to discuss whether any tensions in that arena might have influenced his decision to step away.

Could you come into the station this week?

Regards,

D.S. Elise Monroe

I stare at the screen.

Of course, of course she would smell blood the instant Lang entered the arena.

From her point of view, the story is crystallising into something thorny: a powerful man with enemies, a potentially stolen book, a ghostwriter cut out of profits, and then a vanishing.

If I were her, I'd be circling me, too.

I run a hand through my hair.

Think.

If Lang goes for Marcus hard, if he paints him as a thief, Monroe gets motive: Lang wants revenge, Marcus flees prosecution.

That helps me.

But if she digs too deeply into Marcus's notes, communications, laptop, well, dammit, that hurts me.

I need to steer her.

Give her enough to chase the Lang angle without ever connecting it back to me.

The irony is brutal. I built *The Lattice* to show how power moves invisibly.

Now I have to move myself the same way.

I open a blank document and begin drafting possible answers to Monroe's future questions.

Yes, Marcus mentioned rivals.

No, he never named Lang as a specific threat.

Yes, he was arrogant enough to think he could outplay them.

No, I saw no explicit threats.

Truth.

Laced with omission.

My new specialty.

Later, I stand on my balcony, watching the city glitter.

A book I wrote is being fought over by men who treat billions like poker chips.

One of those men is dead, and one of those men wants to claim ownership.

And I am the only person alive who knows exactly what's in every line, and exactly what was paid, and by whom, to get it into this shape.

Crap, my façade is under pressure. Legal pressure, media pressure, and investigative pressure.

We're not at the breaking point yet.

But I can feel the system straining.

The Lattice isn't just an architecture of tax avoidance; it is a freaking architecture of risk.

Everyone connected to it is now at risk.

Marcus thought he could design a system that allowed the ultra-rich to vanish their money.

I have designed something else: a system where he vanished.

Now I have to ensure that when all of this collapses, and it will, one way or another and somehow, I am the only piece of structure left standing.

CHAPTER 16

The Digital Ghost

There are two kinds of panic.

The first is immediate, loud, and overwhelming. Your body lights up like a fire alarm.

The second is slower.

Colder.

It feels like standing in a quiet room where something is dripping in another part of the house, and you don't know where, or what, or how much.

The message I get from Julian is that second kind.

No sirens, just dread.

Call me ASAP.

No punctuation. No emojis. No tone.

I call him immediately.

He answers on the first ring.

'Okay,' he says breathlessly, 'don't freak out.'

'Don't freak out.' Easy for him to say, I think to myself.

The two most useless words in the English language.

'What happened?'

There's a brief silence.

Then he says: 'Marcus's laptop is back.'

For a moment, I don't understand the sentence.

'Back,' I repeat blankly. 'What do you mean, back?'

'It was turned over to the police this morning.'

My pulse spikes.

'And?'

'And' Julian cuts in, strained, 'the tech unit pulled encrypted partitions. They found partial wipe attempts.'

I sit down.

'Partial. Not full?'

'Not full,' he confirms. 'Fragments. Deleted data. Scraps.'

My mouth dries out completely.

Fragments are worse than full files because fragments force them to look.

'So, what did they find?' I ask.

Julian inhales.

'You need to come in. Now. They want you present when they show us the preliminary.'

He doesn't have to clarify who they are.

Police, the forensic unit, and the publisher's counsel.

I check the clock.

8:14 AM.

'Where?'

'Office. Thirty minutes.'

We hang up.

I shower out of obligation, not necessity, because functioning humans arrive clean, composed, and rational to meetings where their freedom may evaporate.

Clothes: dark pants, a muted blouse, and no jewellery. Just a minimalist and unremarkable, almost invisible look.

As I dress, an image presses into my mind: Marcus's laptop is 'alive.'

I thought I had cleaned it. I am sure I did very carefully, very methodically but I must have cleaned the wrong portions.

Because I didn't know he had an encrypted partition system beneath the boot layer. This is something only someone drowning in paranoia would hide under another hidden system. Marcus taught me every threat model except the one that mattered.

His own.

When I enter the publisher's boardroom, it feels like a courtroom dressed in modern furniture.

Julian is there, and so is Hannah, legal counsel.

A tech forensic analyst sits at the far side of the table, a woman in her forties with short grey hair and steel-rimmed glasses.

Laptop open.

Wires everywhere.

Several connected drives.

Detective Sergeant Elise Monroe stands beside her.

Arms crossed and her expression neutral, and that neutrality is a blade.

'Ms Sterling,' Monroe says.

I nod with exactly the right amount of calm.

'Sergeant.'

There's no seat assigned to me, but Julian gestures sharply to the chair beside him, and I sit.

Hannah launches first, professionally brisk.

'Detective Monroe asked us to be present for the initial review of data fragments recovered from Mr Vayne's computer.'

A small icy drop falls into my stomach, but I keep my face still.

Monroe nods at the forensic analyst.

'Eleanor?'

The analyst types, screen reflected in her glasses.

'So,' she says, clinically, 'the laptop shows two separate wipe attempts. One of the visible drives. One on an encrypted volume.'

'Meaning?' I ask.

She glances up.

'Meaning someone tried very hard to remove data.'

Every pore in my body opens.

'But' she continues, turning the laptop around so we can see the monitor, 'erasure was incomplete.'

I stare at lines of recovered files, not full files, not readable files, just fragments.

But fragments can damn you.

Eleanor explains: 'We have partial email headers, metadata, local file caches, and PDF preview remnants. No full documents. Very readable pages, not much but enough to reconstruct patterns.'

Patterns.

That word carries weight.

'And those patterns suggest,' Eleanor continues, 'that the manuscript had multiple authors.'

Silence hits like a blunt object.

I force myself not to tense.

Hannah speaks first.

'Multiple authors?'

'Or' Eleanor says, clicking open a fragment, 'one primary author and one researcher. Possibly both.'

I exhale slowly through my nose.

Because that is safer than inhaling sharply.

Monroe steps closer.

'What gave you that indication?'

Eleanor taps.

'Draft versions show two distinct writing signatures.'

Julian furrows his brow.

'Writing signatures?'

'With writing software,' Eleanor clarifies, 'each user has subtle data fingerprints. Stylistic patterns in sentence structure, pacing, vocabulary clusters, keystroke metrics. Some writing tools store compressed predictive-text caches. These can persist even after deletion.'

My mind processes every word slowly.

'If two different people worked on the same file, the predictive model shifts. Especially if one person edits or rewrites the other's work. That transition leaves an imprint.'

'So, what exactly did you find?' Hannah asks.

Eleanor brings up a digital forensic graph.

Two colour lines, one blue and the other green, and both distinct.

'Blue is the dominant signature. Almost all the main sections.'

My heart stops.

Blue is me.

'And green,' she continues, 'appears sporadically. Fewer sections. Mostly isolated sentences. Some comments. Some overwritten suggestions.'

Green is Marcus.

'But here's the issue,' Eleanor adds, eyes narrowing slightly, 'there's a third cluster.'

Not blue, not green. A third colour appears on the legend: yellow.

Another writing signature.

'What does that mean?' Julian asks, voice tight.

'It means,' Eleanor says slowly, 'someone besides Mr Vayne and Ms Sterling contributed to the text.'

Julian turns to me, alarm sharp in his eyes.

'I know nothing about that,' I say immediately.

Truthfully.

Because if Marcus had someone else involved before me, or feeding information to him, I would never have known.

Hannah leans forward.

'Are you certain?' she asks Eleanor.

'Data strongly suggests,' Eleanor replies, 'a third contributor. Possibly early on. Possibly someone who provided raw text or structural notes.'

Monroe watches me, measuring.

'You didn't know this?' she asks.

I shake my head.

'No.'

Not a lie.

A surprising blessing.

Hannah pivots.

'We would need to identify this individual,' she says.

Eleanor nods.

'If other hands shaped this manuscript, we have to determine where that input came from. Especially given Lang's claims.'

I control my breathing.

Because this moment is critical. If I look manipulative: dangerous; if I look defensive: suspicious; if I look surprised but composed: credible.

Finally, I ask: 'What do you need from me?'

Eleanor answers.

'Was anyone else involved in the research?'

I think.

Strategically.

Not too long.

Then: 'Marcus sometimes referenced material given to him by consultants. I don't know their names.'

She types.

'Do you have email? Notes?'

'Yes,' I say. 'On my system. I archived everything.'

Hannah seizes on it.

'We can provide those.'

Then, calmly: 'Under counsel supervision.'

Monroe's eyes narrow barely.

Her expression is that of a woman who just spotted the tail end of a mouse disappearing beneath a cupboard.

I ask: 'Is this urgent?'

Eleanor replies:

'If the third signature belongs to someone connected to the Lang allegations, their involvement could constitute collusion. If it belongs to an unknown party, it complicates narrative ownership. If it belongs to an entity with a motive to disappear, Vayne...'

She stops.

The sentence finishes itself.

Monroe crosses her arms.

'The more we understand who touched this book,' she says lightly, 'the clearer the picture becomes.'

The implications are who had motive, who had access, who had knowledge and who had opportunity.

Each word, another tightening thread.

She's not chasing where he went; crap, she's chasing who wanted him gone.

I speak gently.

'If someone else was involved, then we all need to know who they were. I want this clarified just as much as you do.'

The truth of that lands beautifully.

Because she believes it, because I made it sound altruistic, because it sounds practical and mainly because, in a sense, it is true.

Knowledge = control.

And I will need control to survive this.

Monroe studies me a moment longer.

Then nods once.

'We'll coordinate with your counsel,' she says. 'I may have follow-up questions.'

'I'm available,' I reply calmly.

She gives a tight smile, respectful.

Then she leaves.

When the conference room door closes, the atmosphere shifts, and everyone exhales as if someone cracked a window.

Julian collapses back into his chair.

'Well,' he mutters, 'fuck.'

Hannah rubs her temples.

'Third signature complicates everything.'

'It could be nothing,' I offer.

'Someone Marcus hired early, unofficially. Someone disposable.'

Hannah nods slowly.

'Or someone dangerous.'

We all know she means Lang.

Julian's knee bounces uncontrollably.

'This is going to blow up bigger,' he murmurs.

'Press, legal, police...'

'Let it,' I say, in the quietest voice imaginable.

Both of them look at me.

'I can defend the work,' I continue.

'I can explain it. Guide the conversation. Anyone else trying to claim authorship falls apart under scrutiny. I don't fear comparison.'

That lands exactly how I intend. It shows that I am strong, that I am capable and that I am essential.

Julian exhales.

'Good,' he says. 'Because this is far from over.'

He isn't wrong.

But he's wrong about one thing: who this is far from.

Because Marcus is gone and I am still here.

By the time I get home, the sun is sliding low and orange over the suburban rooftops.

I sit on my balcony.

Glass of water in hand.

Not wine this time. I need clarity tonight. I need absolute clarity. I replay the meeting. Go over the forensic data. The third writing trail. The freaking digital ghost.

Someone else's fingerprints, someone who could be leveraged, blamed and weaponised.

Someone who can absorb suspicion.

Instead of me.

That is the opportunity because every system has pressure valves, every structure has a release point, and every lattice needs a weak link.

Someone who can vanish into the abyss of blame both slowly and deliberately,

I open my notebook, and I write three words: *identify third author.*

Then beneath it: *eliminate trail, eliminate the digital evidence, eliminate recognition, and eliminate narrative connection.*

Not by destroying it.

Instead, I will redirect them to someone real. Someone plausible, someone who wanted Marcus ruined, someone the world would believe capable.

I flip to a fresh page and write a name.

Not mine, not Victor Lang but another name.

A new one.

Someone real. Dangerous enough to believe, expendable enough to sacrifice, someone whose fingerprints on the manuscript will make perfect sense to law enforcement because he left a mess Marcus couldn't hide.

And because no one will weep when he is destroyed.

I sit very still.

The page gleams in the fading light.

And I understand something new about myself: I'm no longer simply erasing Marcus. I'm editing the future, line by line, scene by scene and character by character.

Because ghosts don't just disappear, people do.

Ghosts leave a path behind them.

And when the light finally dies, the evidence dies with it.

CHAPTER 17

Closing the Loop

There are two kinds of loose ends.

The ones everyone can see and the ones only you know are dangerous.

The forensic team discovering a third writing 'signature' on Marcus's laptop made one thing clear: there *is* a loose end.

A real one.

A living one.

Someone whose fingerprints, digital or otherwise, touched the manuscript *before* I ever entered the picture.

Someone Marcus trusted briefly, then discarded ruthlessly.

Someone with just enough proximity to be useful and just enough resentment to be manipulated.

When I found his name on an old chain of forwarded drafts, buried in metadata from early working documents, it hit me with the same quiet certainty as a sniper finding their mark.

Evan Marsh, a former junior analyst, a former temporary editorial assistant, a former nobody, and current grudge-holder.

Exactly what I need.

Evan works at a co-working space in Surry Hills, renting one of those sad little desks wedged between a kombucha tap and a mural about 'Hustle Culture.'

I find him hunched over a laptop plastered with stickers about blockchain, productivity, and obscure indie bands.

He looks exactly like the sort of man Marcus would have chewed up and spat out without a second thought.

He is thin and nervous, with hands that flutter too much.

Eyes that dart like he's waiting for fate to hit him with another disappointment.

Perfect.

I approach quietly.

'Evan Marsh?'

He jumps as if I've tasered him.

'Uh, yeah?'

'My name is Anya Sterling,' I say, extending a hand.

Recognition dawns slowly on his face.

'Oh! You're the writer. The ghost—um—sorry; the author of *The Lattice*.'

His correction warms me unexpectedly.

The author—yes, that's who I am now. I think to myself.

'I was hoping to talk to you,' I say.

His brows knit.

'About what?'

'About Marcus Vayne.'

He freezes.

A flicker crosses his face. Fear, guilt, irritation, all fighting for dominance.

He swallows.

'He's missing,' he whispers.

His voice holds no shock.

Just the tone of someone who's been expecting a knock on his door.

Which means he knows something.

This will be easier than I thought.

'Can we talk somewhere private?' I ask gently.

He hesitates, terrified and curious at the same time and desperate for someone to finally acknowledge what he knows.

He nods.

'There's a meeting room upstairs. It's usually empty.'

Perfect.

The room is small, glass-walled, lit by a single overhead pendant. The air smells faintly of stale coffee and carpet cleaner.

We sit across from each other.

Evan's leg bounces uncontrollably under the table.

I calmly fold my hands delicately and let him see my composure and crave it.

'I know you used to work with Marcus,' I begin.

'A long time ago,' he mutters. 'Barely counts. He fired me.'

'Why?'

He laughs bitterly.

'Why not? He fired everyone. Or pushed them out. Or made them miserable enough to quit.'

Good. Bitterness is leverage.

I lean forward, my voice soft.

'You said he fired you because of something to do with the manuscript, right?'

He blinks rapidly.

'You know about that?'

'Yes,' I lie smoothly. 'I found remnants in the document history. I recognised your writing signature.'

His eyes widen.

'Writing signature? That's a thing?'

'It is,' I say solemnly. 'The police found it too.'

He goes pale.

'Am I in trouble?'

I shake my head.

'Not unless you've kept quiet about something you shouldn't have.'

Evan absorbs that with the weight of a man who has been afraid of himself for too long.

He whispers: 'I stole nothing.'

That's all I need.

Fear + innocence = confession.

Gently, I say: 'Evan, I'm not here to accuse you. I'm here because Marcus left a mess. And he might drag you into it.'

He pushes his hands into his hair.

'I knew it,' he muttered.

'I knew something bad was going to happen to him.'

I let the silence stretch, open and inviting, and he fills it.

'He was getting paranoid,' Evan says.

'Before he fired me. Talking about people trying to sabotage him. Competitors. Regulators. Investors.' He said. 'If the lawsuit hits, he'd... he'd disappear.'

I raise my eyebrows slowly.

'A lawsuit?'

Evan nods hard.

'He said Lang was sniffing around. Accusing him of stealing proprietary structures. He said if Lang made it formal, he'd "let the world think he'd gone off grid" until things cooled down.'

My pulse speeds up, but my face stays composed.

This is golden, and real and organic—just perfect and completely outside anything I engineered.

Marcus had been planning to flee long before he vanished.

I can use this. All of it.

'Evan,' I say gently, 'are you saying Marcus said he would disappear to avoid litigation?'

'Yes,' he whispers. 'He said they'd never find him. That he'd live better without his name anyway.'

God bless Marcus and his inflated ego.

He wrote his own exit note.

'Did you ever tell anyone?' I ask.

'No. I thought he was just venting.'

I almost smile, for this is perfect.

I soften my expression.

'I'm going to be completely honest with you,' I say.

He leans in.

'Marcus is gone.'

He swallows.

'I know.'

'No,' I say quietly, 'I mean gone, really gone. He left behind more wreckage than any of us expected.'

'I did nothing,' Evan whispers again, panic tightening his throat.

'And I'm not saying you did,' I reassure him.

'But if the police dig into the manuscript history and see your digital fingerprint, they will ask questions about your role.'

He looks sick.

I continue, tone compassionate.

'And if they learn Marcus talked to you about fleeing litigation, they'll want your testimony. They'll need clarity. They'll need context. And you'll need protection.'

'Protection?' he chokes. 'From whom?'

'From being treated like you helped Marcus disappear.'

His face crumples.

'No, that's not, I didn't, he didn't involve me—'

'I know,' I say, firm but gentle.

He nods rapidly, grateful and grabbing onto the certainty I'm giving him.

I let my hand rest on the table, open-palmed.

'We can help each other,' I say softly.

'I want the truth preserved. You want your name clear. If we work together, we can make sure the police understand

Marcus planned this. That he talked about leaving. That he used people, like you and me, and then walked away.'

Evan stares at me.

He sees sympathy, kindness, and validation, but what he doesn't see is my calculation.

'I want to do the right thing,' he says finally.

'Good,' I whisper. 'Then let's do that.'

We spent the next hour crafting the statement.

Not word for word—not coached—just guided.

I ask gentle questions, and he answers with more emotion each time.

He reveals emails I never knew existed. Emails Marcus sent him late at night, paranoid, and rambling.

Half-written chapters with weirdly aggressive feedback.

And then the gold: A chain in which Marcus complains Lang is 'circling like a vulture,' threatening litigation, and that if the case proceeds, he'd 'rather let the world believe he's on a beach in Malta than spend another second dealing with regulators.'

I almost laugh.

The man literally wrote his own disappearance manifesto.

And Evan never deleted the emails because Evan never expected to matter.

When he finishes telling me everything, he looks relieved, like a man unburdened.

'Will you come with me when I talk to the police?' he asks quietly.

I place a gentle hand on his forearm.

'I'll be right there.'

He exhales shakily.

'Thank you,' he whispers. 'You're the only person who actually cares what happens to me.'

I smile softly.

He thinks it's empathy, but it is my strategy.

But compassion makes manipulation so much easier.

The next day at the station, I sit beside Evan as he gives his statement.

Detective Sergeant Monroe watches him with a predator's patience.

She asks pointed questions.

He answers with honest fear.

He tells her everything: the paranoia, the legal threats, the rants, the plans to flee, the 'I'll disappear before I let them screw me.'

Monroe listens. Silent, absorbing, mapping.

When he finishes, she thanks him.

Calmly and professionally.

Then she asks: 'And you're certain Marcus implied he might vanish?'

Evan nods vigorously.

'Yes. He said it more than once. He said, the lawsuits were coming.'

Monroe studies him.

Then, she glances at me.

Something in her calculation changes.

I can feel it.

When Evan leaves the room, shaking but relieved, Monroe keeps me back with a tilt of her head.

'Helpful,' she whispers.

'Evan wanted to clear his conscience,' I reply.

'You encouraged him?'

'Yes,' I say simply.

She leans back.

'He seems genuinely frightened.'

'He always was, around Marcus.'

'And you?' she asks softly.

'Was I frightened of Marcus?' I repeat, smiling faintly. 'I respected him. And I survived him. That's different.'

Monroe's eyes don't blink.

'Did he ever mention disappearing to you?'

I consider it, craft the answer, and deliver it cleanly.

'He said he needed a break. Time away. But he didn't share the details.'

Monroe taps her pen.

'Funny,' she says. 'People who plan to vanish rarely tell multiple people.'

I tilt my head.

'You think he lied to Evan?'

Monroe doesn't answer. She's thinking, thinking very hard.

'It doesn't change the pattern,' I add gently.

'A man afraid of lawsuits might flee.'

Monroe closes her notebook slowly.

'You're right,' she says. 'It is a pattern.'

Then she stands.

'We'll be in touch.'

A dismissal, a warning and what felt like a promise.

Outside the station, Evan looks at me with raw gratitude.

'Thank you,' he says quietly. 'I couldn't have done that alone.'

'You did the right thing,' I say.

'You don't think they'll blame me, do you?'

'No,' I tell him gently. 'You've helped them. You've helped me. You've helped the truth.'

He exhales and then he walks away.

A small man with a big secret now firmly assigned to someone else's box.

He will never know how much danger he was in; he will never know how useful he has been; he will never know how beautifully he closed the loop around Marcus's disappearance or how perfectly his words now protect me.

I watch him disappear into the afternoon crowd.

Then I turn and walk in the other direction.

Calm, composed and victorious.

Because now, the official story is no longer mine to tell.

It belongs to the police, the publisher, and it belongs to Lang's legal nightmare.

And it belongs to Evan Marsh, the former assistant, who believes Marcus faked his own disappearance to avoid litigation.

I didn't just close the loop I damn well rewrote the loop.

And every time Detective Sergeant Elise Monroe reads Evan's statement, she will follow the trail exactly where I placed it—away from me and straight into the story Marcus created himself.

The perfect alibi, built from truth and polished with some pretty good lies.

Authenticated by the one person who never realised he held the match that could burn me down.

I take a breath.

The loop is closed, and the ghost survives.

CHAPTER 18

The Premiere Deal

There are moments in a life—rare, crystalline—when the world pivots beneath your feet and you realise you are standing on a stage you were never supposed to reach.

For me, that moment arrives in a glass conference room atop a Los Angeles high-rise, sunlight burning through floor-to-ceiling windows, the Hollywood Hills sprawled outside like they're bowing to me.

It doesn't feel real; it feels like a hallucination oxygenated by jet lag.

But the contract in front of me is real, and the pen in my hand is real.

The number at the top of the page is an incredible $200 million (plus backend participation; escalators; merchandising verticals; streaming rights; documentary tie-ins) is real.

The room is crowded with executives, producers, studio legal teams, agents, PR consultants.

All smiling, all hungry and all eager to shake the hand of the woman who wrote the financial thriller of the decade.

The woman who 'exposed' a system so elegant and horrifying that Forbes called me:

'The most important financial storyteller since Michael Lewis.'

If only they knew the actual story.

'Ready?' the lead producer asks, grinning like a shark in an Armani suit.

I smile back, I nod, I sign.

Flashbulbs pop, camera shutters click and applause erupts.

Julian leans over and whispers, 'You just joined the one percent of the one percent as the woman who *nearly* brought them down.'

I grin because that's the story the world knows.

And the story the world adores.

But beneath the applause, beneath the champagne, beneath the California sunlight warming my skin, something else coils inside me.

A pressure like a damn whisper.

Detective Sergeant Elise Monroe. She isn't finished. Not even close.

The party after the signing takes place at a rooftop lounge overlooking the ocean. Producers circle me like satellites; agents make promises hotter than the heat lamps; executives speak to me with reverence, as though I'm holding a grenade made of gold.

It's intoxicating, and it's catastrophic.

A woman from Variety interviews me with breathless enthusiasm.

'What inspired *The Lattice*?' she asks.

When I answer, it is smooth, rehearsed, believable; the words sound like they belong to someone else.

'It was about lifting a veil,' I say.

'Showing the public how the ultra-wealthy stay untouchable.'

She beams.

'And why do you think the world reacted so strongly? The pre-orders alone are staggering.'

'Because we all sense the truth,' I say softly. 'But sensing and seeing are different. The book gave shape to the suspicion.'

Questions spin around me.

Film adaptations, casting, global tour, international rights.

My name floats over the rooftop like something luminous.

But underneath it all, a single thought pulses: Monroe knows the shape of lies.

She's touched the periphery of the truth; she's tugging at seams, and she's not going away.

Later, in my hotel suite overlooking the shimmering grid of Los Angeles at night, with champagne half-finished on the table, I sit on the bed with my phone in hand.

There are three missed calls from Julian, five messages from the publisher and, to top that, a congratulations text from a foreign rights agent.

And one message that makes my stomach drop to my knees.

Damn freaking Detective Sergeant Elise Monroe

We need to schedule a follow-up interview. Please confirm availability within 48 hours.

Nothing else. It has no warmth, no soft edge, no signal of intention, just a precise, clinical summons.

Like a knife left on a doorstep.

I stare at the message.

A cold sweat creeps over my skin. She's speeding up, and the pressure is increasing.

Why now?

Why this week?

I swipe open her last message before this one.

A request for clarification regarding the timeline of my last meeting with Marcus. The nature of our contract dispute (which she shouldn't even know about) and the role of Evan Marsh and the existence of additional contributors. Finally, Marcus's mental state and any 'unusual communications' in the final week.

She is no longer circling, dammit; she is narrowing.

I close the messages, inhale, and tell myself: *She can't catch you. She has only fragments.*

Fragments aren't evidence; fragments are shadows, and I've manipulated the shadows perfectly.

Panic sits behind my ribs like a coiled spring.

Because if Monroe is pushing harder, it means she has something or thinks she does.

And that means I need to move faster.

Julian bursts into the suite twenty minutes later, breathless, eyes wide.

He stops when he sees my face.

'Oh God,' he says. 'What happened?'

I hand him the phone silently. He reads the message, and his jaw tenses.

'Shit.'

'Yes,' I say.

'This is fine,' he insists too quickly. 'Detectives always follow up.'

'Not like this.'

He looks at me.

'Is there something new? Something she found?'

He's asking like a friend, like someone who believes in me.

The cruel thing is he does.

And I need him to keep believing.

'No,' I say softly. 'Nothing new. But she's digging deeper. I can feel it.'

Julian runs a hand through his hair.

'She can't pin anything on you. You did nothing,' he insists.

'I know.' I say as I give him a hollow smile.

But he hears something in my tone, something unsaid.

He sits beside me on the bed.

'Hey,' he says, quieter.

'You're safe. We're safe. This is noise. You're about to be the biggest name in financial nonfiction. They're making a prestige series out of your book.'

I nod and I let him comfort me.

But inside, panic gnaws at the calm surface of my mind like teeth.

Not because I fear being caught but because I fear Monroe won't stop until she convinces herself there is something to catch.

I underestimated her, and that's my mistake, and I cannot afford mistakes, not now.

Not when the entire world is about to watch me become the face of a global franchise.

Not when cameras flash my smile onto screens across continents.

Not when every article reads: *Anya Sterling—the woman who exposed the system the rich fear most.*

Not when the ink on the contract that makes me wealthier than Marcus ever intended to let me be is still drying.

I turn to Julian.

'Can you get me the earliest flight back to Sydney tomorrow?'

He blinks.

'But the studio wants interviews.'

'They can wait.'

'What do I tell them?'

'Tell them I need to prepare properly before the media onslaught. Tell them I'm grounded. Strategic. Serious about accuracy.'

He nods.

'Okay.'

'And Julian?'

'Yeah?'

'Don't tell anyone about Monroe's message. No one.'

He hesitates.

Then nods again.

'You're scared,' he whispers.

I meet his gaze.

'No,' I reply.

'It's worse than that.'

He doesn't ask what I mean. Maybe he should, and maybe he doesn't want to know.

When he leaves, I stand by the window, staring out at the glowing sprawl of Los Angeles.

A place built on myth and reinvention, a city that devours truth and worships story, and for the first time since Marcus vanished, I understand something: The more powerful I become, the more dangerous Monroe will see me as.

The richer I become, the more motive she'll assign me.

The bigger the book gets, the bigger my shadow becomes.

And shadows are where investigators go hunting.

I breathe in and slowly breathe out.

I place my hands on the glass, feeling its coolness seep into my bones.

Tomorrow, I fly home, and I will step back into the territory where Monroe is waiting. Tomorrow the questions will intensify, and tomorrow, the game becomes survival.

But tonight, I stare at the city. At the neon. At the luxury and at the future I stole back from a dead man.

And I whisper to myself: 'You've got everything you wanted, Anya.'

Then, softer: 'Now don't lose it.'

Because I can feel it like a storm building on the edge of a horizon.

Monroe is coming, and this time, she's not circling.

She's hunting for me.

CHAPTER 19

The Final Inquiry

Detective Sergeant Elise Monroe does not summon me politely this time.

She orders me.

A clipped email.

A follow-up call I do not take.

A voicemail with no warmth, just authority.

Ms Sterling, you are required at the station at 10 a.m. Tomorrow for a final round of questioning regarding the disappearance of Marcus Vayne. This is a formal request. Do not delay.

It feels like a knife carefully slid under a rib.

When I walk into the police station the next morning, jet-lagged, hair tied back, spine straight, dressed in a white blouse sharp enough to look honest, there is no illusion left in me.

I feel Monroe wants to break me; she wants to *see* the fracture; she wants to find the seam of guilt and pry it open, but she can only break what she can reach.

And I have buried my truth so deep even I can barely touch it.

The interrogation room is colder than I remember.

A metal table with two chairs, one camera and one woman becoming increasingly dangerous to my life.

Monroe enters with a file so thick it could kill someone if dropped from a balcony.

'Ms Sterling,' she says. Not a trace of friendliness.

'Detective,' I reply, calm.

She sits and opens the file but doesn't look at me yet.

'You've had a busy few weeks, I see.'

I don't answer so that the silence gives her nothing to read.

She flips a page and then looks up.

Her gaze is sharp, focused, and surgical.

'Let's begin.'

I calmly fold my hands in my lap.

'Of course.'

She starts with a map.

A literal map.

Laid flat across the metal table. A timeline of Marcus's last known movements. Sightings. Phone pings. Receipts. Emails.

With straight lines, curved arrows, and lots of question marks.

'At first,' she says, tapping the map, 'this looked like a standard missing-person case. A wealthy man wants privacy. Disconnects. Leaves.'

She taps again.

A harder strike.

'But some things don't add up.'

I meet her eyes, giving her a quiet invitation.

'Such as?'

Monroe slides a photo forward and shows me a photo of me and Marcus at the harbour bar.

Captured by a tourist in the background of a selfie two tables over.

She watches me carefully.

'You were the last confirmed person to see him alive.'

I nod.

'Yes.'

'You didn't seem distressed.'

She flips the photo to a blown-up crop of my face.

'You seem calm. Happy, even.'

'I had just finished the biggest project of my life,' I say gently. 'I had no reason to be distressed.'

She nods once and then the attack shifts.

'You said Marcus was triumphant that night.'

'He was.'

'And you also said he seemed like someone who was preparing to step away.'

She slides forward with my earlier statement.

My words. Neutral. Perfectly controlled and now weaponised against me.

'Preparation for success and preparation for retreat are contradictory states,' she says.

'Not for Marcus,' I reply. 'He believed he could do both.'

She leans back.

'You're very confident in your answers.'

'I'm confident of the truth.'

'You don't stutter.'

'I don't lie.'

She studies me for several long seconds.

Then: 'I think you're lying.'

My pulse flares. Tiny but very contained.

But I hold her gaze evenly.

'Then please show me the lie.'

Her mouth twitches.

Approval or irritation?

Hard to tell.

She turns another page.

'I spoke with Evan Marsh again.'

The temperature in the room drops.

'He said you encouraged him to tell us everything.'

'Yes,' I say. 'Because he seemed scared. And because he deserved clarity.'

Monroe folds her hands.

'And because his testimony paints Marcus as paranoid, planning to flee litigation, and talking about disappearing.'

'Yes,' I say, steady. 'Because that is the truth.'

She taps her pen.

Quietly, rhythmically, like a blade being sharpened.

'Convenient,' she murmurs.

'For whom?' I ask.

'For you.'

I let a small frown crease my brow.

'What would be convenient for me?'

'That Marcus fled,' she says bluntly.

'That he left you holding the book. He disappeared to avoid lawsuits. That he abandoned everything.'

'That's not convenient,' I say.

'That's tragic.'

She watches me.

'You expect me to believe you didn't want any of this?'

I take a soft and controlled breath.

'Detective Monroe, I wanted recognition. I wanted fairness. I wanted my work acknowledged. I didn't want a man to vanish.'

She tilts her head.

'Are you sure?'

A long pause hangs between us.

Then, she pushes another document across the table.

An airline manifest. Private flight. Sydney to Cayman Islands. Departure: two days after Marcus's last confirmed sighting. Boarding list: three crew and one unnamed passenger.

And something else: a transfer authorisation for creative rights signed digitally from Marcus's encrypted key.

My throat tightens, but not from panic, but from awe.

This is the beauty of building a disappearance around truth.

Not every detail must be fabricated.

Sometimes, if you put them in the right order, the truth arranges itself exactly where you need it to go.

I lean forward.

'Where did you get this?'

'A subpoena to the private aviation lounge,' she says. 'Your name appears nowhere. But Marcus's code was used. Same one registered for his other international movements.'

I nod slowly.

'It seems he always planned to flee.'

Monroe folds her arms.

'Someone could have used his identity.'

'Someone could have,' I say. 'But why would they? What would they gain?'

She hesitates. She doesn't have a suitable answer.

I continue, voice steady.

'That flight was paid for using his offshore account. The same one he used to withdraw funds in the days before he vanished.'

She flips through the pages.

'Yes,' she admits.

'And the rights transfer?' I ask quietly.

She stares at the paper.

The digitally signed contract. Date-stamped before he disappeared. It assigns secondary rights to me. Clean, legal, and binding.

'Did he tell you he planned to give you the rights?' she asks.

'No.' And I let the vulnerability show.

'He blindsided me with it.'

Her brows lift.

Micro-expression.

Important.

'Blindsided?'

'Yes. I was told I'd get nothing. That all rights were his. That I had no future in the project. And then, suddenly, he transferred everything to me. I assumed it was his guilt catching up to him.'

I look down at my hands.

Let my voice soften.

Let humanity slip in.

'The last conversation we had was awful, Detective. I thought he wanted to cut me out forever. And now it looks like he was making amends before he left.'

Something flickers in Monroe.

Not sympathy but understanding.

The worst thing for an investigator to feel because understanding erodes suspicion.

She exhales slowly and in a measured, tired manner.

'What do you think happened to him?' she asks.

Not accusing me.

In asking me, I look up and meet her gaze evenly.

'I think he ran,' I say. 'From Lang. From the lawsuits. From everything. He always believed he was smarter than everyone else. Disappearing would look like victory to a man like him.'

Monroe nods slowly, almost reluctantly, because the story fits, because the evidence supports it and because her instincts, sharp as they are, cannot pierce the narrative I have laid like a trap around every fact she holds.

She closes the file.

Just closes it.

The sound is small, but it feels enormous—like a verdict, a concession, like a surrender wrapped in professionalism.

'Ms Sterling,' she says, voice softening by one degree, 'at this time, there is insufficient evidence to support any criminal suspicion related to you or your involvement in Mr Vayne's disappearance.'

She looks pained as she says it because detectives hate the absence of closure, sometimes more than they hate crime.

'I have to close the case,' she finishes.

I inhale slowly, and my entire body relaxes by only the width of a breath, but it is enough.

'Thank you,' I whisper.

As Monroe stands, I do as well.

She offers her hand, and I take it.

Her grip is firm, grounded and human.

'Just so you know,' she says quietly, 'my instincts still don't like any of this.'

I smile gently.

'Instincts aren't evidence.'

'No,' she says, releasing my hand, 'but they're what get me out of bed.'

'Then I hope they lead you somewhere good,' I reply.

Her eyes search mine.

For what? A crack? A confession? A flicker of guilt?

She finds nothing.

Because I have become exactly what I needed to be: a woman with impeccable logic and impeccable paperwork and impeccable calm.

A woman who tells only truths that lead away from danger.

Finally, Monroe nods once.

Reluctant but respectful and defeated.

'This interview is concluded,' she says.

Then she leaves the room.

The door closes behind her with a quiet click.

I stand alone for a moment.

Breathing. I feel alive, free and something inside me, something dark and triumphant and terrifying in its purity, spills out slowly.

The case is closed.

Marcus is officially gone, and I am officially the survivor, the truth-teller.

The wronged party turned visionary author, standing on the brink of global fame and extraordinary wealth.

I pick up my bag and walk out of the station and step into the sunlight.

And I whisper to myself: 'You did it.'

Then: 'You're untouchable now.'

But as I cross the street, I feel the faintest shadow at my back.

Not a threat but a reminder.

Detective Monroe didn't believe me; she simply lost her war, and an instinct like hers doesn't disappear, it lingers. It is watching and waiting.

Hunting for a seam that doesn't exist.

I smile.

Let her hunt.

There is nothing left to be found.

Marcus is gone.

And the ghost who erased him has become a legend.

Epilogue — Detective Monroe

I close the case file on Marcus Vayne at 2:47 p.m. on a grey Wednesday afternoon.

The room smells of dust and old coffee.

The stale air where critical decisions linger.

The official recommendation reads:

Case closed. The subject likely fled the jurisdiction to avoid financial litigation. No evidence of foul play.

My signature sits at the bottom of the page.

Final. Permanent. Legal and wrong.

I lean back in my chair and stare at the ceiling.

Something is off.

Not enough to reopen anything. Not enough to write a memo. Not enough to accuse.

Just enough to rot quietly in my mind like a splinter buried too deep to remove.

Anya Sterling.

She walked out of the last interview clean, calm, and polished. Every answer just plausible enough. Every explanation is just human enough.

Every truth was wrapped so neatly in coincidence that challenging it felt like chasing smoke. She didn't flinch. She didn't hedge. She didn't panic.

But she *wasn't innocent.*

I don't mean guilty of murder.

Not necessarily.

But innocent people talk differently.

They reach for the truth, fumbling, messy, emotional.

Anya reached for precision.

Like someone editing her own thoughts before they ever touched the air, like someone who knows what narrative sounds best, and like someone who understands story structure too well to let real life go off script.

I tap the case file lightly with my fingertips.

A quiet drumbeat.

Something is wrong here, but I cannot prove it.

And I don't chase ghosts without proof.

Not anymore.

Not after 2019.

Not after the case I still wake up remembering.

A missing woman, whose husband smiled too easily. A trail that looked perfect until it wasn't. A truth I uncovered too late.

I told myself that would never happen again.

Yet here I am, letting another disappearance slip through my fingers.

I close my eyes. Marcus Vayne's face flashes behind my eyelids.

Smug. Arrogant. Armed with the kind of confidence only obscene wealth can buy.

Men like him don't simply vanish. Not cleanly. Not without noise and not without loose ends.

Unless someone helped them or someone *stopped* them.

I shake the thought off.

There's no body. No blood. No motive that holds legally. No evidence.

Only instinct and instincts don't win cases.

A soft knock interrupts my thoughts.

'Detective?'

I open my eyes.

Constable Hammond stands in the doorway, holding a tablet and looking hesitant.

'What is it?' I ask.

'There's, um... something you might want to see.'

I frown.

She sets the tablet on my desk and presses play.

A news clip opens: Anya Sterling stepping onto a red carpet in London, cameras flashing, wearing a gown that probably costs more than my entire yearly salary.

A reporter off-camera shouts: 'Anya! Anya! Any comment on rumours the franchise could reach two billion worldwide?'

Anya smiles for the camera, radiant and impossible to read.

Then the clip cuts to an interview.

The reporter asks: 'Do you think Marcus Vayne will ever resurface?'

Anya gives a polished, soft, carefully rehearsed answer—the kind meant to sound noble, wistful, tragic.

'I believe Marcus made his choice,' she says.

'And the world is moving on.'

I freeze the video.

Zoom in on her expression.

There's something in her eyes.

Not grief, for sure not uncertainty but something sharper, more private as if it felt victorious.

A silent sentence hiding behind the smile.

Something she isn't saying. Something she never will.

My jaw tightens.

'What made you show me this?' I ask Hammond.

She shrugs uneasily.

'I don't know. The way she said it... it felt off.'

A pause.

'You always tell me to trust my instincts.'

I stare at the frozen image.

Anya Sterling. The woman the world now worships. The woman who walked free.

And I think: *She knows something.*

Not enough to catch her.

But enough to haunt me.

'Do you want me to flag anything?' Hammond asks.

I shake my head.

'No, it's closed.'

'Are you sure?'

My hesitation lasts half a second.

Too long.

'Yes,' I say. 'Case is closed.'

She nods reluctantly and leaves.

The room goes silent again. Too silent.

Because I know myself.

I know what this silence means.

It means this isn't over.

I hover my cursor over the 'Archived Cases' folder.

For a long moment, I consider dragging Marcus's file into it.

Let it disappear into digital storage forever.

But I don't.

Instead, I create a new folder.

Untitled. Then I rename it: VAYNE—ADDITIONAL NOTES.

It isn't formal. It isn't authorised. It isn't even investigative.

It's instinct.

And instinct, in the absence of evidence, is a dangerous thing to feed.

Inside the folder, I drop a single document.

Just one line, typed in plain black text:

Sterling knows more. Revisit when something cracks.

I close the file.

Close my computer.

Grab my coat.

But as I walk out of the station, one truth pulses behind my ribs like a heartbeat: *Something about Anya Sterling doesn't fit.*

And I have never forgotten a case that didn't fit.

They follow me. They find me. They will eventually reveal themselves to me again.

It might be weeks. Months, maybe years.

But the truth has a way of rising.

And when it does, I will be waiting.

I step into the evening air.

Cold. Sharp. Full of possibility.

The city hums its restless song under a bruised sky.

Somewhere in the world, Anya Sterling is celebrating her coronation as a mogul.

Somewhere, cameras are flashing. Somewhere, champagne is pouring. Somewhere, she's whispering something triumphant into the dark.

And somewhere beneath that, quiet and stubborn as a pulse, I feel the case pulling at me again.

A whisper I cannot unhear.

A ghost refusing to stay buried.

I lock my car, slide into the driver's seat, and start the engine.

As the radio crackles to life, I say aloud, not to the air, not to myself, but to the ghost of the questions still unanswered: 'This might not be over, Ms Sterling.'

Then I drive into the night.

Straight toward whatever comes next.

ABOUT THE AUTHOR

José F. Nodar is an Australian Cuban author, reviewer, and literary entrepreneur based in Spring Farm, NSW. He is the founder of Quick Story Tales Online and World Book Reviews, initiatives supporting and promoting both emerging and established authors worldwide.

José's writing blends humour, sentiment, and quiet realism, often drawing from the landscapes and community spirit of regional New South Wales. His fiction, including Whispers from My Wife, The Northport Coffee Group, and Stories to Share with My Partner Collection, explores universal themes of love, loss, and rediscovery.

When not writing, José can be found reading at a local café, walking along Spring Farm's footpaths, or championing local authors and creative groups through interviews and newsletters.

Please visit https://worldbookreviews.com.au/ and let me know what you thought of this book of short stories and poetry.

Good, bad, or indifferent, I will always welcome your honest opinion.
Send me an email at info@jfnodar.com.au

Thank you for your purchase!

Other books by José F. Nodar:

Novels in English

The Danny Monk Trilogy

Books, Pens & Larceny
Mending Hearts at Crystal Cove
A Love Finally Spoken

The Mallard E. Benson Trilogy

The Girl Who Didn't Come Home
The Ones That Got Away
The Ghost We Owe

Mystery

The Ghost Detective's First Case
The Northport Coffee Group

Romance

The Teacher's Assistant
A Night of Love
Maybe This Is Everything
Love in Stereo
When Love Remembers

Science Fiction & Fantasy

The Compass Legacy
The Universe Between Us
The Time Bus
The Last Light of Aurethis

Children

The Hamster Who Whispered Back

Humour

SEX

Collections of Stories and Poetry

Stories to Share with My Partner Book 1
Stories to Share with My Partner Book 2
Stories to Share with My Partner Book 3
Stories to Share with My Partner Book 4
Stories to Share with My Partner Book 5
Stories to Share with My Partner Book 6
Stories to Share with My Partner Book 7
Stories to Share with My Partner Book 8
Stories to Share with My Partner Book 9
Stories to Share with My Partner Book 10
Stories to Share with My Partner Book 11
Stories to Share with My Partner Book 12

Anthologies of Stories and Poetry

Quick Stories & Poems Volume I
Quick Stories & Poems Volume 2
Quick Stories & Poems Volume 3

Libros en Español

La Trilogía de Danny Monk

Un Amor Expresado
Reparando Corazones en Crystal Cove
Un Amor Finalmente Declarado

Colecciones de Cuentos y Poemas

Cuentos Para Compartir con Mi Pareja Libro 1
Cuentos Para Compartir con Mi Pareja Libro 2
Cuentos Para Compartir con Mi Pareja Libro 3

Ciencia Ficción y Fantasía

El Autobús del Tiempo